RUMORS

BY DENYS CAZET

Creston Books

Text and illustrations copyright © 2017 Denys Cazet
Cover and book design by Simon Stahl

CIP data for this book is available from the Library of Congress.

Published by Creston Books, LLC
www.crestonbooks.co

Source of Production: Worzalla Books, Stevens Point, Wisconsin
Printed and bound in the United States of America
1 2 3 4 5

MIX
Paper from
responsible sources
FSC® C002589

FSC
www.fsc.org

RUMORS

BY DENYS CAZET

An Observation Concerning Certain Rumors

There is an old rumor that crocodiles live in the sewers under the streets of New York City. Flushed away when little through fear of what they might become when big, they've grown fat on the family pets that have "passed on" in the apartments and condos of the city. Roaming the sewers and pipes, they feed on goldfish, hamsters, and pink-eyed mice that have been given a prayerful farewell and then swooshed away in a swirl of sadness into the dark world beneath us.

There are rumors of other creatures traveling through the miles of piped highways under buildings, and not just in big cities either. For instance, the Napa Register reported that Stacie Hoops, age eleven, a student at Robert Louis Stevenson Middle School, found a salamander the size of a Chihuahua sleeping in her bathroom shower.

How did it get there?

Pipes.

On July 15 the Apache Creek Sentinel reported on a local lawsuit filed by Bob and Ethel Stanley against the owners of the E-Z Gas and Quick Stop on Highway 60, near Pie Town, New Mexico.

According to the article, when Mrs. Stanley came out of the ladies' room she was followed by a swarm of stink beetles that picked up their Honda Civic and carried it away, along with the family dog, a Shih Tzu named Sweetie.

And in the September 9 issue of the Gallstone Gazette, there was a short article on Duane Kronk, president of All Glue Prefab Homes. The article said that while Mr. Kronk was demonstrating the durability of the aluminum siding to a group of interested buyers, one of the clients' children, Maxwell Parrott, age 11, went inside to use the bathroom. Six witnesses say they heard a flushing noise followed by a whoosh and then saw a ball of corn snakes shoot out of a vent pipe.

Really?

Travel by pipe?

Hard to believe!

The whole idea of things traveling in the pipes under a house, under a school, is ridiculous, preposterous, and just plain silly.

Isn't it?

1

Show and Tell

After Tony finished clearing his throat and blowing his nose, he stuffed the soggy handkerchief into his back pocket. "Pipes," he said solemnly. He paused to let the word sink in.

"Pipes."

He studied the class a moment and then sighed. "My sister," he announced, "is down the drain. I found out about it last night!"

The only person not paying attention to Tony was our teacher, Miss Butters, Miss Mable Butters. She sat at her desk, frantically stamping Friday's classwork with smiley faces, the weekend just minutes away. The papers were flying.

"My father told me," continued Tony. "All I said was, where's Angelina?" Angelina was Tony's twenty-year-old sister. She was the oldest of Tony's brothers and sisters. There were a lot of them.

"Where's Angelina? That's all I said. My father just blew up. I don't mean exploded into little pieces and stuck to the ceiling. I mean turned purple with rage.

"'Where is Angelina?' Papa shouted. 'Where is my darling Angelina? I'll tell you where! Down the drain! That's where!' He ran into the bathroom and turned the faucets on and off, shouting 'DOWN THE DRAIN! Down the drain with that no good, spineless, jelly-boned, lily-livered, pinheaded snake! That slimy, sneaking eel, that burping gas bag, that Pimple-head Charlie!'

"My mom made my father lay down with a cold cloth on his head. He kept muttering, 'Down the drain, forget college, forget the mayor's son, she's down the drain.'

"When I asked my mother if I could have Angelina's room, she burst into tears!"

Tony sighed. He looked out the window at a passing truck loaded with irrigation pipe. He smiled faintly and then looked back at the class. "I think it must have happened while my sister was washing her hands. One minute she was there and the next she was down the drain with Pimple-head Charlie!

"Questions?" Tony asked.

Lindsey Meyers raised her hand.

"Yes?"

"If this Pimple-head Charlie can come up through the sink, how does he get past that S-shaped pipe that's underneath?" She aimed a sly little smile at her best friend, Daniela. Daniela nodded. "How does he get through a pipe that small?"

Lindsey sat down, looking smug. All the girls looked smug. This was a real Tony masterpiece. I couldn't figure out how he was going to polish it off.

"You have a fair knowledge of pipes," Tony said. "The S-shaped pipe you referred to is a drainpipe. My family is in the business, Ragusa Plumbing and Janitorial Supplies. We know our pipes."

Tony looked like he felt sorry for her. "Let me tell you something about pipes," he said gently. He picked up a piece of chalk and stepped up to the blackboard. "Pipes," he repeated.

After a short lecture on pipes of the Roman Empire, Tony began making a list of all the different kinds of pipes there were in the world. There were drainage pipes, water pipes (cold and hot), sewer pipes, vent pipes, heater pipes, and on and on. The list seemed endless. All this time, Tony was drawing examples of pipes and how they were all connected.

"What most people don't realize is that the further away pipes get from your average sink, the larger they become. For instance, in a large city there are miles and miles of pipes that end up under the street. They have to be larger there because collectively—that means together," Tony looked at Butch, "all those smaller pipes are discharging." Tony looked at Slow Eddie and smiled. "That means emptying. So the pipes they dump into must be much larger. Some drain pipes under city streets are big enough to drive a truck through."

We gasped. Who knew? How come Miss Butters never told us about this kind of stuff? All we ever heard about were famous dead people and how important it was to floss.

"So," Tony continued, "as you can see, the problem of getting around in 90% of those pipes is only at the very beginning, or at the end, depending on which way you're moving. The real problem is right here."

Tony tapped the blackboard with his chalk. He circled a drawing of a sink drainpipe. "Here," he said, "where the pipe makes a turn at this elbow."

"Exactly!" Lindsey blurted out. "How does he bend around that angle?"

"Good question. Pimple-head Charlie must be like a jellyfish with arms and legs. That way he can get around those turns pretty easy."

Miss Butters stopped stamping.

Even she was listening.

It was five minutes to three.

Max and Big David, my other best friends, nodded in my direction at the same time. Max tapped on his watch and whispered, "He's eating up the clock!"

Daniela ignored them and raised her hand. She still wasn't convinced.

"Yes?"

"I can see where Pimple-head Charlie the Jell-O Man might be able to get through the pipes but how could he pull your sister down the drain? *She's* not made of Jell-O!"

Tony sighed. "I know. I don't get it either. That part's a mystery..."

"Ha!" Daniela cried out. "Then how do you know she's really down there at all?"

"Yeah!" chortled a chorus of girls.

"I heard her! First the pipes rattled under the house

and then the bathroom sink started making burpy noises—"

"And?"

"And then I heard her," said Tony. "At least it sounded like her."

"From the sink?" Lindsey sounded skeptical.

"No…from the heater vent."

"Was she crying?" Gretchen asked. "Didn't you try to save her? Did you call the police? Didn't you call out to her?"

"Sure," said Tony. "I put my face next to the floor register and called out, 'Is that you, Angelina?'"

"What did she say?"

"She just said what she always says to me."

"What?"

"'Shut up, you little twerp!'"

2
Don't Call Me Sweetheart

When the 3 o'clock bell rang, Max, Big David, and I were all over Tony like a rash, giving him high fives and slaps on the back, laughing all the way out the door.

"What drama!" I shouted.

"The timing was perfect!" said Max. "Not a minute was wasted. Extraordinary!"

"Yeah," agreed Big David. "You made me a believer!"

"What a story!"

"I got to tell you something," said Tony. He looked down at his shoes. "What I said in there—"

"Brilliant!"

"A blockbuster!"

"Fanny-tastic!"

"It was true," said Tony.

Everyone stopped so suddenly that Max tripped and we all stumbled into a heap in front of the old portable at the edge of the Carpy Field playground. Daniela and Lindsey walked by, giggling.

"Walk much?" asked Lindsey. Daniela whispered something we couldn't hear and they both laughed. Ordinarily, I would have said something clever, but I was too stunned to care. All of us were.

"You're kidding," Big David said. "Aren't you?"

Tony shook his head. "No! Everything happened just like I said."

Just then, Ms. Maurer, the After School Reading Club teacher stuck her head out the portable door and called her students into the room.

"I gotta go," said Big David. "We're starting a new reading program today. My grandma says I have to do it."

I looked back at the portable. "What new reading program?"

Big David picked up his backpack. "I don't know. I think it's called Reamed On Phonics. Don't wait for me. I don't know how long it's going to take. I'll see you at the football game on Sunday. My brother is playing and he got us free tickets." He waved and disappeared into the classroom.

Max pounded Tony with questions. "What did you really see? How do you know if…Why didn't you…How come…If your sister was really down the drain, how did…"

"Jeeze, Max, shut up! I told you everything I know!" Tony opened his backpack and took out an apple. "What do you want from me?"

"I was just asking. You don't have to go ballistic. I need information, that's all."

Max was Mr. Information. When something piqued his interest, he wouldn't stop asking questions until he had learned what he wanted to know or we sat on him to shut him up. I had questions myself, but when Tony bounced the apple core off the top of Max's head, I knew better than to say anything. We walked on in silence.

Wouldn't that be something if it was all true? Then again, Tony did tend to stretch the truth a bit. Why should he be any different than the rest of us?

The Ragusa plumbing truck was parked in front of Tony's house.

Max pointed at it. "Your dad's home early."

"Yeah. He's putting in a new garbage disposal for my mother. She's been kind of upset since Pimple-head Charlie went down the drain with Angelina. I'll see you at the game."

He stopped to help his father who was struggling with a heavy cardboard box sitting in the back of the truck. We waved and turned the corner, walking past the house where Big David lived with his grandmother. A couple of dogs barked as we crossed the street to Max's. Max stopped and let his backpack slide off his back and set it by his feet.

"I have a question, I don't see how..."

"I know," I said, holding up both hands. "How is it possible for someone like Angelina to be squeezed down a drain? She wasn't exactly a thin mint."

"So you don't believe it happened?"

"Something happened, I believe that!"

"Do you think Tony was lying?"

How can you answer a question like that without feeling you're letting down one of your best friends? A yes answer sounded disloyal and a no answer sounded...dumb.

"I have questions," said Max, picking an apple seed out of his hair.

"Of course you do."

Max climbed the steps to his front porch.

I stood on the sidewalk watching Max pull the mail out of the mail slot and leaf through the pile. "Any news from Pinesap?"

"Jeeze, Russell, don't you ever forget anything? Do I dwell on your family's quirks?"

"Quirks?"

"Yeah...like your father hauling horse manure in the family sedan!"

"Hey! I was just asking!"

"Hilarious! I'll see you at the game." He went into the house and slammed the door.

Pinesap was the official magazine for a nudist colony in New Hampshire. Every summer Max had to go with his family to the Pinesap Nature Camp. Every time we'd ask Max what it was like, he always said the same thing: "One minute at Pinesap and you think that the best thing God ever did for the human race was to invent clothes."

I crossed through the small park near our house. It was shorter to go right up Olive Street but I loved the smell of the big eucalyptus trees. Of all the seasons, fall was my personal favorite. There was a large round fishpond with a cement fountain in the center of the park. On my worst days, I'd jump on my bike and ride over to watch the goldfish swim in and out of the lily pads. Some days I'd just lie on the grass under one of the old eucalyptus trees. In the winter I liked to be the first to break the ice and watch the goldfish rise to the open surface.

I was still thinking about Tony and Pimple-head Charlie when I got to my house. My father was already home from the bank where he worked. He was outside, still in his suit, watering his garden. He should have been a farmer. When he was in his garden, he was always happy. When he was at the bank, he was always grumpy.

My mother was in the bathroom bathing Annie, my three-year-old sister. With the exception of Annie, I'm an only child.

"You better not get that baby near the drain," I warned. "Stuff happens!"

As soon as Annie saw me she tried to wiggle out of my mother's arms. "Ack, Ack," she cried. "My Ack!" She sounded like the cat coughing up a hairball.

You would think by now she would be able to say my name! "Your brother's name is Russell, Annie, it rhymes with muscle." I flexed so she could see what I was talking about. "No? How about Russ? Can you say Russ?"

"Ack!"

"Annie! Hold still," cried my mother. "You wouldn't need a bath if you'd stay out of the garden and away from your father's manure pile! Sweetheart, hand me that towel."

"Ma, please don't call me that. What if you slip and call me sweetheart in front of one of my friends?"

"Your friends aren't here. Towel, please!"

Annie slid away from my mother and wrapped herself around my leg. She soaked up my pants pretty good. "My Ack!" she said for the billionth time.

"Oh, man," I moaned. "Look at my jeans!" I wrapped a towel around her and picked her up. She put her arms around my neck and hugged me again.

"Ack!"

My mother took her from me and dried her off. "That is so sweet."

"Ma...you were in the hospital for three days. Couldn't you have brought back a puppy? Maybe an iguana?"

"I'm afraid that's not quite how it works," she said. "Go change your pants."

Thanks to my parents, we're a television-deprived family. Meaning, we don't have one. We watch a lot of movies on a monitor with a DVD player. My father is a movie buff and he loves Westerns. Tonight was John Wayne night. His favorite, not mine, so after dinner, I went up to my room.

I tried reading an old issue of *Mad Magazine* from my dad's comic book collection, but my mind kept returning to Angelina Ragusa and Pimple-head Charlie. I could see how Charlie, if he really was like a jelly man, all stretchy and super bendable, might get around in those pipes, but how did he get Angelina down there? There was a lot more to this than any of us understood. Or was there? Maybe Angelina just got sick of junior college and took off with her girlfriends to Mexico to catch some rays. Maybe those burpy noises Tony heard were just the kind of noises old pipes make in a tired old house.

But what if it was true?

I found myself thinking how wonderfully weird this all was. Not the disappearing Angelina part, but a jelly person zipping around underground without the upper world knowing anything about it. Why not? Scientists were always discovering new species in New Guinea or the rainforest, so why not under the Ragusa house?

I must have fallen asleep thinking about it because I had a nightmare that the jelly man was walking around our house looking for Annie.

I sat bolt upright, sweating. My mother was calling Annie's name. The bathroom light went on and I heard her call again.

I jumped out of bed and ran down the hall. The jelly man, Pimple-head Charlie, down the drain with Annie! I skidded to a stop in front of the bathroom door. My heart was pounding! My mother was standing just inside the bathroom.

"There you are. How did you get out of your crib?" Annie was looking at the water swooshing round and round in the toilet bowl.

When Annie saw me, she raised her chubby arms and said, "Up." I picked her up and she pointed at my eyes. Her fat little finger came closer and closer. I closed my eye and she touched my eyelid. "Eye," she said.

She wiggled until I put her down. She went over to the toilet and looked in. She pulled the handle and the water flushed out of the bowl. She watched it disappear. "Eye," she said. "All gone."

3
The Weekend

Eyes in the toilet? I spent the rest of the night taping down toilet lids, closing sink traps and bathtub drains. When I finally did fall asleep, I didn't wake up until nearly noon.

There was a note on the refrigerator door from my mother. She'd gone shopping with Annie. I knew where my father was. I could hear him out in his garden. He was singing *The Hills Are Alive* from *The Sound Of Music* in a high-pitched voice.

"Jeeze," I muttered. "And people think *I'm* weird!"

I poured myself a large bowl of Fruity Loopy's and added a couple of spoons of sugar just to get the adrenaline going. I called Tony to tell him about last night, but I got the Ragusa answering machine. The Ragusas didn't have their kids record a cute message like most families. Instead, the family all sang a commercial for Ragusa Plumbing.

I tried Max and then Big David and got the same results, nada.

So I got dressed and went out into the garden. My father was still singing. Only now he was imitating Judy Garland singing *Over the Rainbow* from *The Wizard of Oz*.

"Dad, please," I begged. "Keep it down. What if one of my friends comes by and hears you?"

"So?" he said, propping up a wayward tomato plant.

"So…it's embarrassing."

My father looked at me for a moment. "I'll tell you what's embarrassing."

"What?"

"Getting up in the middle of the night to use the bathroom and finding out someone has taped the toilet lid closed!"

Sunday morning my mother made my favorite breakfast, chocolate chip Belgian waffles smothered in blackberry syrup.

"What's the matter, sweetheart?" She put her hand on my forehead. "You feel a little warm."

I put down my fork. "Ma, I want to say something about Friday—"

My mother sighed. "Oh, Russell, not another pink slip from Miss Butters. Have you been 'flapping your gums' again?"

"No," I protested. "Well, I mean yes, a few small

flaps maybe, but no, I don't have a pink slip from Miss Butters."

She held a spoon loaded with mashed prune in front of Annie's face. Annie kept moving her lips like a little bird waiting for its morning dose of pre-chewed worm, but the spoon was just out of reach. "It's a note from Sunday School, isn't it? Can't you and Tony just sit and listen? Is one hour a week too much to ask for a little enlightenment concerning your moral and ethical standards?"

My father rattled his newspaper.

"There's still hope for your son," my mother said, glaring at the newspaper. She pointed the spoon at me.

"You've been asking questions again at Sunday School and—"

"No, I—"

"Giving funny answers to serious questions?"

"Ma! I—"

"Don't tell me you were sent to the office by the yard teacher again, another little episode with Ms. Krunchensnap, the principal? I knew this was coming. It's been too quiet. What was it this time? Spitting out a ping pong ball, pretending you lost an eye during P.E.?"

"That was Tony!"

"Aiding and abetting, I believe Ms. Krunchensnap called it! Honestly, Russell, Ms. Krunchensnap's black box must be filled with your antics. You and your friends must each have your own box. What's to become of you?"

"He could work in a bank," my father said, safely hidden behind his paper.

"Ma! I just want to tell you what happened to An-

16

gelina Ragusa. Tony said something called Pimple-head Charlie came up through the pipes and snatched her and dragged her down the sink pipe and maybe, just maybe—"

"Oh!" My mother exhaled and relaxed. "Is that all? I heard all about it at the PTA fund-raising meeting. As if anyone could believe such a far-fetched story! Don't worry about something that never happened. The Harvest Festival is just days away. Now that's something to worry about! I still haven't figured out what the main attraction is going to be. It has to be something special, something big, something different, something that will encourage people to spend money for the school." She shoved the spoonful of mashed prune into Annie's mouth.

Annie gulped it down and opened her mouth for more.

"Why don't you have Ms. Krunchensnap wrestle Greta, the butcher's wife?" I suggested.

My father put down his newspaper. "Now that is a great idea!" he exclaimed. "I'd pay to see that! You could—"

My mother pointed a fresh wad of mashed prune at my father. "Don't be disrespectful!" she said. She pointed the spoon back at me. "That goes for you, too!"

"Ma, please, don't point that mess at me." She ignored me and shoved another load of mashed worm into the little bird's beak.

"Ack!" Annie sprayed prune mush all over my shirt.

My mother wiped off Annie's mouth. "You naughty little girl," she said, laughing. "Go change your shirt, sweetheart."

"Oh, man! How come I'm always the one getting

spray-painted with prunes?"

"Why do you think I have this newspaper in front of me?" my father asked. "You think I'm reading it?"

My mother stared hard at the wall of paper. "Mother warned me about marrying someone with witty genes."

My father lowered his newspaper and looked at me. "Never marry a woman with a mother."

"Ma, I just want to tell you about what happened at the Ragusa's because maybe Annie saw the same—"

"I already heard all about it," she said, dabbing the corners of the little bird's beak with a damp washcloth. "Now go change your shirt. Put on the light blue dress shirt that just came back from the cleaners. It's on your bed. I had it starched."

Did she ever! Putting on that shirt was like trying to put on a cardboard box. I was afraid if I lowered my arms, the sleeves would break off with my arms still inside them.

By the time I got outside to the car, my neck felt like it had been rubbed raw by one of those industrial sand blasters Tony and I saw last summer removing stucco from the old library building.

"You look very nice," my mother said. "Why are you holding your arms out like that?"

"Because there's so much starch in this shirt, I can't lower them."

"Don't be silly. You look nice and crisp."

My father was putting the rear seat back in our brown '72 Malibu. Every time he got a load of dried horse manure for his garden, he crammed as many sacks as he could into the trunk and the back of the car. It smelled for weeks.

"I'm not getting in there," I announced. "I don't want to smell like a horse stall that hasn't been cleaned since the horse died."

"I vacuumed it out," said my father. "And see, I hung a couple of those pine fresheners on the door handles. It smells fine."

My mother put Annie in her car seat and made me get in the back.

"You could hang a whole pine tree in here and it'd still stink," I complained.

"Open your window!" my father suggested.

My mother glared at me. She was almost as good at glaring as Krunchensnap. "Don't be rude, young man. Maybe 'Mr. Flapping-his-gums-a-little-too-often' should stay home from the football game today and wash a few windows!"

I hung my head out the window like Rosy, the Ragusa's cocker spaniel, all the way to church.

As we sat down, I saw Mrs. Mac, the priest's wife, glaring suspiciously in my family's direction. She was probably wondering where that fresh garden smell was coming from. It's coming from over here, I wanted to shout, the Pepe Le Pew family.

By the time we got home, there was only a half hour before I was supposed to meet Big David. I changed into a T-shirt and left in a rush, but I was still late. The game was getting ready to start and I couldn't get in without a ticket. Jeeze. What else could go wrong?

"About time," someone said. It was Max. "We've

been taking turns waiting for you. Man, what's that smell?" He handed me a ticket. "Has your father been hauling manure in the Malibu again?"

"Bingo!"

As we walked to the stands, I told Max about Friday night and the disappearing eye.

"Annie's only a baby," he said. "What could she have seen?"

"I'm not sure."

"Don't tell me you think this eely Charlie was..." Max stopped and grabbed my arm. "Hey, you know what? Last night we were watching *Big Time Wrestling* in the family room when some glasses fell from the shelf that's over the sink. At first I thought it was Tickles. But maybe it wasn't."

Tickles is Max's 18-year-old cat. He weighs in at 42 pounds, bigger than Rosy, the dog. In fact, there isn't a dog in the neighborhood that doesn't cross the street to avoid him.

"It wasn't the cat?"

"Now I'm not so sure. Tickles was staring at the sink. His back was arched, his hair was sticking straight up, and he was hissing. The drain screen was lying on the floor."

I started to say something but was drowned out by the referee's whistle and the roar of the crowd. We sat down next to Tony, Big David, and his grandmother.

"Man! What's that smell?" Tony complained. "Has your father been hauling—"

"Yeah, yeah!"

Grandma David gave us all hugs and pinches. "My boys!" she chirped. She opened up a huge picnic basket that was filled to the brim. "I don't want my boys getting hungry!"

"This is Grandma's first game," Big David explained.

"I came to see my Little David play his feets ball!"

"Football," Big David corrected.

Little David towered over the other players on the field. He was called Little David because when he was born he only weighed three and a half pounds. Now he weighed two hundred and eight pounds and was six foot seven. When his younger brother was born, he weighed ten pounds fourteen ounces. At least that's what Grandma David said.

When Little David spotted his grandmother sitting behind his team bench, he waved. Grandma David blew him some kisses. She reached into the picnic basket and took out a salami the size of a bazooka and a long loaf of French bread.

"Grandma," said Big David. "What are you doing?"

"I'm going to make Little David a sandwich. He looks so thin. I'll make some for you boys, too."

Grandma David was one of the kindest people I knew. She took in every stray dog and cat in the neighborhood. She was always repairing some bird's broken wing or nursing a wayward squirrel back to health.

I don't know why everybody was named David in their family. Even the grandma was called Grandma David. She was only about five feet tall and wispy thin. On hot days she had something cold for us to drink and on cold days she made bowls of soup that she called "bone warmers." She loved her boys but she was strict, too. If the brothers got into trouble, she made them get a chair so she could stand on it and wag her angry finger in their faces. Big David called it "getting the chair."

I never asked Big David where his mother and father were and he never brought the subject up. There were a lot of family photographs on the wall, on the mantel, and the piano, just about everywhere you looked. Maybe one of them showed Big David's mom and dad but I never asked.

Suddenly, there were whistles blowing everywhere. The crowd was screaming and Big David was shouting, "Grandma! Come back!"

"What happened?"

"Didn't you see that?" Tony asked.

"Little David just intercepted the ball!" said Max. "He's hanging on to it at the bottom of that pile of St. Sebastian players!"

At the top of the pile, Grandma David was pounding on the helmet of one of the big offensive guards from St. Sebastian with the big salami.

4

Where There's Smoke

Two coaches, four referees, the high school principal, and Police Chief McCormick, who was Gretchen's dad,
were all out on the field, trying to convince Grandma David
to stop hitting the offensive guard with the salami.

Finally Little David emerged from the pile and
pulled up the offensive guard. The guard shook his head,
spit out a divot of turf, and trotted back to the line of scrim-
mage.

"Grandma David," said Chief McCormick, "you
have to get off the field."

"Did you see what those boys in the purple shirts
did to my Little David? They pushed him down and tried
to take his ball away. Nobody picks on my Little David and
gets away with it!"

Little David escorted his grandmother across the field. "Grandma," he said gently. "It's okay. This is the way the game is played. I'm fine. Stay in your seat. Big David will explain the rules to you."

Grandma David noticed the St. Sebastian players watching her as she walked off the field. She stopped and pointed at them with the salami. "You're lucky I didn't bring my chair," she shouted.

The crowd applauded. The cheerleaders gave Grandma David a "Who Do We Appreciate" cheer. The fans in the bleachers, including many of the St. Sebastian supporters, joined in. The only ones not cheering were sitting at the very top of the stands, Butch and Slow Eddie.

Little David ran back on the field and said something to the coach. The coach laughed, the referees blew their whistles, and the game continued. Grandma settled in next to Big David and opened up the picnic basket again. She took out another salami.

"Thank goodness," she said, as though she had never left her seat, "I packed a spare. Who wants a sandwich?"

We all did. Grandma made sandwiches for everyone, including the row of fans behind us.

Meanwhile, Little David was plowing up the field. Every time the quarterback handed him the ball, Little David gained fifteen to twenty yards. On the last play, he crossed the goal line dragging three players from St. Sebastian's behind him.

"I'm going to the bathroom," Max announced.

Big David stood up. "I'll go with you." He looked at me, then at Tony. "Keep an eye on things." He nodded towards his grandmother. Tony and I scooted closer to her. She seemed content to watch the game now that Big David had explained the rules to her.

When Max and Big David returned, they both looked like they'd seen a ghost.

"What's the matter?" Tony asked.

"That was one of the weirdest things I've ever seen," whispered Max. "If I really did see it."

Big David shook his head. "I saw it, and I still don't believe it. Some kid was sitting on the bathroom roof, watching the game. I shouted at him to get down before he fell."

"Did he fall?"

"Not exactly...he jumped!"

"Off the roof?"

Max stared off into space, rerunning the impossibility of what he thought he had just seen. He took a deep breath and said, "No. He, it, jumped down the vent pipe!"

"A vent pipe is only two to three inches wide. How could... Guys, it's him!" I shouted. "Come on!"

Tony was already running toward the bathroom.

"Stay with Grandma," I said to Big David. "Max, come on!"

Tony waited for us by the bathroom door. He put one finger on his lips. "Shhh, he could be inside right now."

"Tony," I whispered, "I changed my mind. This is crazy. Maybe we should tell Gretchen's dad. I don't..."

"I saw what I saw," said Max.

"What if he's a biter?" I asked nervously.

"Bite him back!" Tony snapped.

"Okay, okay." What was the use in arguing about

something if your best friends ignore you anyway?

Tony raised his hand. "Slow down! Let's try to sur-prise him. Which vent pipe did he go down?"

Max pointed to the right of the building.

"Are you guys nuts? That's the girls' side!" If they heard me, they didn't pay any attention. So what else was new?

We dropped down behind some shrubs and silently worked our way along the outside wall. We tried to make ourselves as small as possible, which was easy for me since I'm only at the 75% mark on Dr. Meyers' growth chart. Tony signaled us to stop at the door. We listened. There was a flushing sound and a very large woman in shorts and a very small T-shirt came out of the bathroom. She stopped and stared at us.

"You boys weren't peeking, were you?" One of her plucked eyebrows rose high above the other. "Hmmm?"

Tony smiled, looking up at the sign above the door. "Oh, gosh, looks like we're on the wrong side!"

The lady winked and waddled away.

"She'll never have to worry about disappearing down a pipe," I muttered.

"Shhh," whispered Tony.

We slipped into the bathroom. No one else was there. Thank goodness for small favors. Without making a sound, Tony pointed toward the stalls and Max moved to that side of the room. Tony and I crept closer to the sinks. The pipes under the bathroom floor began to rattle and the sinks made burpy noises. Tony squeezed my arm and point-ed at the middle sink. The chrome stopper at the bottom was moving. Slowly it slid up and fell out of the drain hole. We peeked over the edge.

An eye looked out of the hole.

"Mind your own beeswax," said a tight little voice.

"JEEZE!" I yelled and jumped back.

Tony shoved me aside, grabbed the exposed drain-pipe under the sink and yanked as hard as he could.

The pipe came off. Greenish feet stuck out of one end and a bald head popped out of the other.

The bald head screamed.

More screams came from two of the stalls behind us.

"I got him!" Tony shouted just as Lindsey came out of one of the stalls and Daniela came out of the other. They both started screaming again when Tony lost his grip on the pipe and it bounced across the tile floor. The weirdest looking thing I'd ever seen shot out of the pipe, straight into the air, all wiggly and panicky, and scrambled towards the stalls.

"Pimple-head Charlie!" I yelped.

"Snake!" Lindsey cried.

"He's going for the toilets. Close the lids!" Tony ordered. Max spun around and ran into Lindsey. They both yelled. A stall door slammed and there was a splash. We all picked ourselves up and stared into the empty stall.

Gone.

"Well, well, well," said a deep voice from the door-way. "What do we have here?"

It was Ms. Krunchensnap, the school principal.

"Three boys in the girls' bathroom with two girls, or is it two girls in the girls' bathroom with three boys? How odd."

She began circling us like an overweight tiger around a herd of gnus. She rolled her shoulders and cracked her knuckles. Was the rumor about her true? Max had told us that she was a retired professional mud-wrestling champion. He said she was called Big Mama the Eye Popper.

Ms. Krunchensnap whipped out a notepad so suddenly we all jumped back and gasped at the same time. "Well?" she demanded.

In a magnanimous gesture I stepped forward. "It's re-re- really my fault," I stuttered in my humblest tone. "I..."

"I never thought otherwise," snapped Krunchensnap. "I am a little surprised at you two girls. But that's what happens when you hang around with boys in the girls' bathroom! Yes, a very serious offense."

Lindsey began to cry. "This so humiliating. What if people in town hear about this? My father's a doctor."

Daniela glared at me.

"These girls are innocent!" I cried. I tried to remember a scene from one of my father's Westerns. A small group of calves surrounded by cattle rustlers came to mind. John Wayne walked right up to the leader and said, "Let these innocent calves go and I'll let you keep your old mules."

"What kind of nonsense is that?" snarled Krunchensnap. She wrote all of our names on the notepad. Daniela was furious. Lindsey looked like she was ready to burst into tears.

"Now as to why you are all in here—" Krunchensnap stopped. She sniffed the air. She inhaled deeply. "Oh," she said, walking around the bathroom. "I smell something. Dried hay. A grassy smell, a tobacco smell," she said, smiling.

"Have we been smoking something?"

"Smoking!" said Tony, indignantly. "We were chasing Pimple-head Charlie to get my sister back! Lindsey and Daniela just happened to be here."

"Your sister, Angelina," she smirked. "Yes, well, I heard all about her. But you know what they say." She sniffed the air again. "Where there's smoke, there's fire. Tell the truth. What were you smoking?"

"Manure," Max blurted out.

"What?"

Tony glanced at Max, an odd look on his face. "Manure?"

Max nodded and gestured toward me.

"Oh, yeah, manure!" Tony repeated. "Manure. Russell was showing us how to roll our own manure cigars. If you don't believe me just take a whiff of him."

"I knew you were the instigator of this little party." She leaned forward and began sniffing. "Ahhh," she said. "Yes, Mr. Sprout, I do detect a rather pungent essence."

She turned and looked out of the open door to the clear blue sky beyond. "So sad," she lamented, raising her eyes to heaven, "when they start so young."

I could see Butch and Slow Eddie standing on the other side of the field giving each other high fives.

Krunchensnap pointed at us. "I will see you all in my office at noon tomorrow!"

5
High Noon

The sky was slate gray, heavy and frozen over our classroom like a sheet of cold plate steel waiting to fall.

Except for the occasional glare from Daniela and a sniff or two from Lindsey, the six of us were pretty quiet. The whole classroom was quiet. Except for Miss Butters. She flitted from desk to desk, helping the less fortunate with their math. She seemed a bit too jovial for a Monday morning, especially this Monday morning. Had she no respect for those of us about to take the long walk at high noon? Joe Asher, the custodian, must have put a new battery in the wall clock. It was moving a lot faster than usual.

Even Big David was gloomy. He told us before school started that Little David had been pulled from the game because his grandmother felt sick. An ambulance came and the coach let him ride to the hospital with her. She was back home again, resting with a new heart prescription from Dr. Meyers. We could tell Big David was still worried.

I looked at the clock. Fifteen minutes past eleven. Forty-five minutes to high noon, but who was counting?

"Psst," a voice whispered.

I looked up. It was Butch.

"What?"

Butch cracked a crooked smile. "I heard the rumor."

"What rumor?"

"I heard you guys was fooling around in the girls' bathroom with certain girls." He looked over at Daniela and Lindsey and winked. "And got busted for smoking."

Daniela's shoulders hunched up. She turned slowly and looked him right in the eye. "That's a lie," she snarled.

Butch smothered a laugh into his shirtsleeve. He held up his hands in mock defense. "Hey, it's just a rumor. It's what I heard, right, Eddie?"

"Right," agreed Slow Eddie. "Did you hear the rumor about old lady David croaking…"

Now I'm going to try to describe what happened in the next split second. I know it will sound impossible, but it actually happened. I don't know how he did it—maybe he was fired out of an invisible cannon—but Big David exploded out of his desk and shot across Daniela's without ever touching the floor. You could almost feel the heat and smell the smoke as he blasted straight across the room into Slow Eddie's face.

Big David dropped him like a brick.

The next thing we knew, Butch jumped on Big David, and Tony jumped on Butch. Lindsey and Gretchen were holding onto Daniela, afraid she was going to jump in next.

A startled Miss Butters kept clapping her hands for attention. "Boys! Boys!" she shouted. "Boys! Stop it this minute!" She pulled them all apart. "What is the matter with you?"

"Gee, Miss Butters," whined Slow Eddie. "All I said was, 'How's your grandma, David,' and he punched me." He touched his eye. "Man, that hurts. He gave me a black eye, Miss Butters."

"Yeah," added Butch. "We was just kinda concerned for her welfare on account of her being on her death bed and all. We was motivated by kindness, Miss Butters."

Miss Butters picked up a notepad from her desk and wrote Eddie's name on it. "Here," she said. "Take this to the office and have Mrs. Wu put some ice on your eye."

"Thank you, Miss Butters. Am I going to lose my eye? Cause Butch's dad is a lawyer and we wouldn't want to have to sue, you know, like for pain and suffering for the loss of an eye, or something." He squinted at Butch and asked, "How much for an eye?"

"More than an ear," said Butch knowingly. "And a lot more than for an arm or a leg."

Slow Eddie nodded thoughtfully and left the room.

Miss Butters shook her head at Big David. "This is the third time you've been in a fight. I'm afraid, young man, you're going to have to join Russell and his accomplices when they go to the principal's office." She handed Big David a note.

David never took his eyes off Butch. He was giving Butch the death-wish squint and Butch didn't like it one bit.

"Teacher," Butch complained, "David is looking at me!"

"David," said Miss Butters. "Fighting won't solve anything!"

"I don't like what he said about my grandmother."

"Is she feeling better?"

Big David nodded. "She's home. Dr. Meyers said her medication was too strong, so he changed it."

"See. All's well that ends well."

Miss Butters sighed and sat down at her desk. She took out a small mirror from her purse, adjusted her hair, and put on some fresh lipstick. She unfolded a small piece of paper, smiled, and then put it back in the purse. "Time for your appointment," she said, tapping her watch. "Take your backpacks. You might be there a while."

David snatched up his backpack, turned and gave Butch one last laser death stare, and then followed us into the hallway. We walked silently to the green room where rumor had it Krunchensnap kept an electric chair and her pet gorilla, Kong.

6

The Chamber of Death

We stood in front of the office door. There was a window at the top of the door and we could see Mrs. P, the school secretary, talking on the phone. Her full name was Ponchettavonatraki or something like that. It was so hard to pronounce that everybody called her Mrs. P. She could be very funny, and she seemed to be especially fond of all the oddballs in the school. She liked me a lot.

When she saw us, she waved us in, pointed at the chairs lining the wall, and put her hand over the phone. She looked into the hallway to see if there were any more of us. "Do you want me to see if I can get you a group rate?" She gave us a little smirk and went back to the phone.

"No," she continued. "Only the one. Looks like they came in through the window, broken glass everywhere.

Don't know, everything was locked up as usual. The police chief is in there with Ms. K right now. Are you kidding? I'd hate to be the next one in her office...I'd rather..." Mrs. P saw us sitting in a row, staring at her, wide-eyed. "Gotta go!"

She hung up and took Big David's note. She glanced into the back room and then at Big David.

Mrs. P's helper, Ms. Wu, was putting an ice pack on Slow Eddie's eye. "Did you do that?"

Big David looked down and shrugged, embarrassed.

"Nice shot," she said, handing the note back. The intercom buzzed. "Yes, Ms. Krunchensnap? They're sitting right here. Yes, they were on time. No, I won't turn my back on them. Would you like me to check for guns, knives, rocket launchers—no, Ms. Krunchensnap, you're right, that wasn't funny. No, I wouldn't want Ms. Wu to have my job. Thank you, Ms. Krunchensnap." Mrs. P set the phone down and stuck out her tongue. She looked at us. "You didn't see that, did you?"

We all shook our heads. Some of us had been here once before, okay, more than once, but even I had never been into the inner office, her office, Ms. K's office, the office of no return, the chamber of death.

"She'll let you know when she wants you to come in. And Russell, come here." I got up and leaned over the counter. "Remember the class mural you worked on for Public Schools Week, the one about ancient Egypt and the building of the pyramids? You drew kindergartners pushing huge blocks of stone up a ramp with Ms. Krunchensnap whipping them."

Oops.

"She knows it was you," said Mrs. P. "Just because you signed Butch Johnson's name to the picture doesn't mean anyone believed Butch was that good of an artist."

I looked at Max, Mr. I-have-an-idea, let's-sign-Butch's-name-to-the-picture. Max was looking out the window at Mr. Asher, the custodian, sweeping up window glass. Thanks, bud, every man for himself!

"You already have two strikes against you, Russell."

"Two?" I asked, almost sincere disbelief in my voice. "What's the other one?"

"Telling Slow Eddie that if he held his breath and jumped off the tool shed, he would float down," she said. "Slow Eddie told Ms. Krunchensnap it was you!"

"Me?" I looked at Tony. He looked away and began to hum an old tune called *I Hear You Knocking But You Can't Come In.*

"The black box is open," Mrs. P continued. "She is not in a good mood. Someone broke into her office last night and stole her Mud Wrestling Champion of the Century trophy. Watch what you say. Practice a little humility."

So it was true. No rumor.

Suddenly, a deep booming voice spewed out of the loudspeaker. "YOU MAY ENTER!" bellowed the voice and the door swung open on its own.

We got up as one body with twelve legs. I felt like we should be chanting, "Lions, tigers, and bears, OH MY!" I expected to see a giant, flaming Krunchensnap head floating in the middle of the room.

What a disappointment. The room was small and

painted an industrial green. No electric chair. At least not one I could see. There was another door in the room, and I wondered if that was where she kept Kong, the gorilla she liked to arm-wrestle to keep in shape.

One wall was lined with glass cabinets that were filled with wrestling trophies. Some of the trophies were huge. On the opposite wall, mixed in with her certificates and degrees, were pictures of the Madison Square Garden marquee with her name in big letters: "Krunchensnap the Eye Popper."

On the back wall a large bulletin board was covered with notes, school district policies, and a pages-long wish list of hundreds of new school rules she wanted enacted next year. Below the bulletin board stood a cot with a pillow and a single wool blanket.

The wall behind us was empty except for a cabinet. There was a green felt cloth on the cabinet shelf but nothing else.

Next to the case, half in shadow, stood Police Chief McCormick, Gretchen's dad. He leaned against the wall, twirling his handcuffs.

Whoa, I thought. Krunchensnap called the police because we were in the girls' bathroom? For smoking? We all huddled on the other side of the room. Any closer to each other and we would have been standing in each others' pockets.

Krunchensnap was on the phone. She put her hand over it and ordered us to sit down. There were no other chairs in the room so we sat on the floor in front of the chief.

"Because I forgot, that's why!" she snapped at someone. "I need someone in there to sub for her right now. I can't leave the kids in the room unsupervised. They're bad enough when the teacher is in the room. You think I want some parent suing me?" She slammed down the phone and looked back at the chief. "Well?"

"Well?" said the chief. "Are these the suspects?"

Lindsey burst into tears. "It wasn't my fault," she cried. "I was minding my own business when these boys came in, chasing a giant boa constrictor that was smoking a cigar. No, I mean the snake—"

"What snake?" asked the chief.

"She's delirious," said Krunchensnap. "Probably the result of all those cigars they were smoking! I blame those boys...they're always up to something."

Lindsey fell on one knee. "Have mercy!" she begged.

"Whoa!" said the Chief. "I'm only here to check out the break-in. Anything else, smoking or non-smoking, is in the principal's jurisdiction!"

Ms. K straightened her back, rolling her shoulders as she stood. "I want my trophy back!"

"Yes, ma'am." The chief hurried out, closing the door behind him. We all breathed a sigh of relief. It sounded like a chorus of flat tires.

"Stand up!" bellowed Ms. K.

We stood.

Krunchensnap cracked her knuckles. She looked at Lindsey, who was trying to fade into the wall. "Minding your own business," she sneered, shaking her head in bitter disappointment. "And you," she pointed at Daniela. "The winner of the spelling bee five years in a row. Hanging out with these, these..."

The phone rang and she snatched it up.

"Now what? Where? The teacher's bathroom? The sink? Well, put them in a bag and send them up. I already told you to get a sub for her! And make it a cheap one!" She hung up.

"Where was I?" She noticed Big David for the first time. "Wait a minute," she said, picking up her notepad. "I don't see your name on my manure list."

Big David handed her the note.

I made my move, stepping toward the trophy case. "Oh," I said, shielding my eyes. "Would you mind closing the shades?"

"What?"

"I'm sorry, Ms. Krunchensnap, the light from the window reflecting off of those brilliant trophies blinded me for a moment. They're beautiful. A collection like this must have cost a fortune. Where did you buy these?"

"Buy?" she snapped. "What are you talking about, you little pinworm?" She got up and opened one of the cabinets, taking out a trophy. "Read that!"

I read out loud: "Intercollegiate National Title First Place Wrestling, Heavyweight Division, 1983, 1984, 1985, 1986, B. Krunchensnap, Champion."

A faint smile cracked her rigid face. "Read that one," she demanded.

"International Collegiate Heavyweight Wrestling, All World Championship, 1983, 1984, 1985, 1986, 1987, 1988, B. Krunchensnap."

Ms. Krunchensnap inhaled proudly and beamed. "Go on," she said with a flick of her wrist.

I moved on to the larger trophies. "Rookie of the Year, World Wrestling Federation, 1983, B. Krunchensnap."

Tony jumped in. "Look at the size of these! Why, these are practically all World Championships."

Then Max. "You must be very proud!"

Even Big David chimed in. "We're so lucky to have a principal like you, Ms. Krunchensnap."

I looked over at Daniela and Lindsey and gestured to them.

"Oh," said Lindsey. "Yes, wonderful." She looked at the empty case and asked nonchalantly, "Why is this case empty, Ms. Krunchensnap? Oh! Is this what was..."

Daniela gave her a look.

"What?" Lindsey whispered.

Ms. Krunchensnap's eyes bulged. She began rolling her shoulders, cracking her knuckles again, and breathing as though she was trying to stifle an eruption. Her shaking finger pointed at the empty case. "Stolen," she growled. "STOLEN!"

We all edged towards the door, one body and twelve legs ready to escape and relieved to see The Eye Popper was too consumed by the theft of her trophy to remember we were there.

There was a knock on the door and Mrs. P came in carrying a shopping bag.

"Here it is," she said, setting the bag on Ms. Krunchensnap's desk.

Ms. Krunchensnap emptied the shopping bag onto her desk. It was full of women's clothes. Miss Butters' clothes!

"Oh," we gasped at the same time, recognizing our teacher's dress.

Mrs. P picked up the shoes. "Should I leave these in her mailbox?"

"No, of course not. I've already taken care of her. What about my trophy? Do you know how much that trophy is worth?" Her head snapped back in our direction. "You had something to do with this, Mr. Spoot! You and your gang!" She tore up David's note and wrote his name on the manure list. "This time I've got you and you're going to help me get my trophy back!"

"How?" I blurted out.

Krunchensnap stared at me and smiled. It wasn't a very nice smile, either.

"You'll see. All of you will! Now, get out!"

7

A Touch of Holiness

Smiling Sally was our substitute teacher. There was a rumor going around that she had been an extra in the making of the movie *Night of the Living Dead*. No one knew her real name, but whenever Miss Butters was gone, she was our sub. She asked us to call her Miss Sally. Her expression never changed. She always sat in the back of the room with a grin locked on her face. Our assignments were written on the front board.

We hadn't heard the verdict for the Manure Crime of the Century, but it was coming. I knew it. We all knew it. The big K was planning something. She liked to let the threat of punishment hang there, her unopened present filled with nasty possibilities.

The week dragged on and on. There was a lot of

classroom talk about the disappearance of Miss Butters. The rumors were flying. No one talked much about the Eye Popper's trophy.

Then on Thursday, Joe Asher, the custodian, disappeared.

"Pimple-head Charlie," said Tony.

"Hey!" said Max. "Maybe Charlie took the Eye Popper's trophy!"

"Now he's breaking into an office and stealing a trophy?" I shook my head. "It doesn't make any sense."

Max scratched his head. "Maybe not. Gretchen told me she heard Mrs. P talking to Mr. Rodriquez, the groundskeeper. She heard him say that he found Mr. Asher's clothes on the floor of his basement office with his shoes in the sink."

"Miss Butters' clothes were found in the sink and now the custodian's. What does that tell you?" Tony asked.

Max shrugged. "Maybe we should start some kind of community service urging people to tape down their toilet lids and stuff."

"Are you serious?" Tony snorted. "What, Lids for Kids?"

I shook my head again. "There's something else going on here and I'm not so sure it has anything to with Pimple-head Charlie."

"What do you mean?" Max asked.

"I mean how do you get a 250-pound man down a sink drain?"

"Grease?" Max suggested.

The three o'clock bell rang, and we walked out

together. Daniela and Lindsey still weren't speaking to us. When we passed them, they looked away at something less loathsome.

We crossed the street and walked down a block to Grace Church where Tony and I had an hour of Sunday School. Why it was called Sunday School when it was on a weekday was beyond my limited understanding of these things.

Big David had brought his basketball so he and Max could enjoy some hoops in the parking lot while we enjoyed our weekly dose of Bible-thumping instruction from Mrs. Mac.

Mrs. Mac was a no-nonsense teacher who loved her subject. Mostly she was grouchy, though Tony claimed to have seen her in Sunshine Market, laughing with some friends in front of the fruit bins. She was partial to the girls. "Boys fool around too much," she would say. "No good can come from too much fooling around. If you want to find the devil, look in the middle of a group of boys who are fooling around."

She was stocky and muscular and short, not much taller than me, and believe me, that's short! She looked a lot like Al Capone's grandmother. She even had a faint mustache.

Tony and I sat down in class. As usual, we were the last ones there.

Mrs. Mac stood in front of us. "Do you two have some kind of fooling-around contest going on?" she asked.

Tony smiled weakly. "What?"

"In the entire year I've been here, I don't think

I have ever seen you two get here before anyone else. You are always last. Makes me think you don't want to be here. Makes me think you'd rather be outside playing basketball with your friends. Makes me think you'd rather be outside, fooling around, challenging the devil to a basketball game of Outs!"

"Never!" said Tony.

"Heaven forbid!" I declared.

"That's why we're here!" she shouted, raising her hands toward the ceiling. "SO!" she continued, addressing our little class of young, weak souls. "Today we'll review the basics. Today the questions are simple. The answers are clear. Genesis. Adam and Eve. The Bible tells us that God made them. So my question to you is: Who made you?"

She began walking up and down the aisles. My head was so busy telling my mouth not to say anything stupid, I didn't notice her walk up behind me and stop. I kept staring at the cross with poor Jesus pinned to it. It looked so painful that I said, "Ow!"

"The answer to who made you is ow?"

"Oh, no, what I meant was..." I looked at Tony for help but he was too busy checking his fingernails for plumbing grease. "I mean, well, do you mean, ah, spiritually or biologically?"

She stared at me and frowned, waiting. "Go on."

"I mean, I don't know a lot about it, but there's the pollywog thingy with the long tail and the egg thingy...and they meet and talk about old times and mutual friends, and the egg thingy says I can see by your cap you're an A's fan and he says, I love that dress..." A quick glance around the room told me that I may have taken a wrong turn. "On the other hand," I continued, "Spiritually—"

"God!" Tony blurted out. About time!

Mrs. Mac turned slowly and stared at Tony, hope in her tired, gray eyes. "And?"

"And, ah, God made us..."

Mrs. Mac leaned closer. "Yes, yes," she said. "God made us in—"

"Nebraska?" I offered.

She squeezed her eyes shut and said to no one in particular, "I'm thinking of a commandment."

"Love thy neighbor?" someone suggested.

"No."

"Thou shalt not kill?" one of the girls shouted out.

"Thank you," said Mrs. Mac politely. "And God made us in…"

"His own image and likeness!" said all the girls in unison.

"Thank the Good Lord for girls," she muttered, looking up at the ceiling. "That will be all for today. Class dismissed."

Tony and I grabbed our backpacks and rushed out the door. "Nebraska?" he said. "Man, you must have some kind of death wish or something. You better watch what you say!"

"I tried," I said defensively. "It just came out!"

"You better learn to shut up or you're never going to make it to high school."

"Hey! It took you long enough to get the answer… more or less!"

"So?"

"Yo!" Big David yelled. "You're out early."

We walked home, talking about Pimple-head Charlie, wondering where he might strike next. Should we tell someone what we saw? Who? Would anyone believe us?

Max asked a lot of questions nobody could answer and Tony finally had to threaten to sit on him to shut him up.

We stopped in front of Big David's house. "Come on over to my house," said Tony. "There's no homework and you could spend the night."

"I think I'd better stay home," Big David said. "Grandma David might need me. She's taking some new medicine."

"You want us to help with something?" I asked.

"No, I'm okay. Thanks."

We waited until he went through the garden gate. Two scruffy-looking dogs began jumping and barking around his legs. He picked them up and they licked his face. He laughed and then closed the gate with his shoulder.

We crossed the street to Max's. "I'll see if it's okay," he said. "You want to call your mom from here, Russell? My cell phone is dead. Then we can go back over to Tony's."

Tony nodded. "Sounds like a plan."

Max checked the mail slot but there was no mail. He opened the front door and stopped. He listened for a moment and then pushed us back out the door.

"What?"

"You can't come in," said Max, his face red. "It's my mother."

"She okay?" I asked, worried.

Max shook his head. "She's vacuuming!"

Tony and I looked at each other and shrugged. "So!"

"Look," said Max. "She likes to vacuum in the nude. Okay!"

"Okay with me," said Tony, peering in the window.

"Hey! Do you mind? That's my mother!"

The door slammed and the window drapes slid closed.

8

A Close Encounter

By the time the three of us walked back to Tony's, it was already starting to get dark. Mrs. Ragusa was on the phone.

"They just walked in," she said, looking at me. "Your mother."

Man, how do they do that? There must be some kind of mom radar or something. They know where you're going even before you get there. My mother wanted to get me a cell phone because "I'd be safer and could call her anytime I needed to." Ha! The real reason was so she could find me quicker. Who needs an electronic leash? I felt the back of my neck to see if there was a lump where she'd buried a tracking chip.

"Russell," repeated Mrs. Ragusa. "Your mother."

"Oh, hi, Mom. What? No, I didn't break into her office and steal her dumb trophy. That was days ago. I was sitting next to you and dad, watching *Tarzan of the Apes!* Who did you think that was sitting next to you, Cheetah the monkey? Jeeze, Ma! Okay, okay. I'm sorry. How do you find out about these things? What kidnapping? Miss Butters? I don't know. Maybe she just changed her clothes and went jogging. We have a sub. No, Ma. Sorry, Ma. Yes, Ma."

An image of us standing in the office flashed through my brain. I remembered getting a glance at Mr. Asher sweeping up the glass outside and Krunchensnap tearing up Big David's note. Something was off. I could see it and then I couldn't. What was it?

My mother's voice floated back into my head. "No, Ma. Nothing's wrong," I heard myself say. "No, Ma, there's no homework. No, I don't have a note from the teacher. No, Mrs. Mac didn't send one either. I think she likes me."

"Tell her about Nebraska," Tony said.

"Shut up!" I moved to a more private corner of the kitchen. "No, Ma, not you, Tony. He was trying to be funny. Is it okay if I stay over and babysit? Max is here, too. Okay. No, we'll be fine. Okay. Bye. I know, Ma. Yes." I lowered my voice. "I love you, too," I whispered. "See you tomorrow."

"What a sweet boy," said Mrs. Ragusa.

"What a sweet boy," repeated Tony.

"What a sweet boy," echoed Max.

"You both could take a lesson here," said Mrs. Ragusa to Tony and Max.

I smiled triumphantly.

Mrs. Ragusa was very organized. Even though Tony's little brothers and sisters were always running in and out of the kitchen, everything was spotless. "Your father's away tonight," she said. "And I have to meet with the PTA fund-raising committee. The Harvest Festival is only a few days away and we still don't have a main event."

"Main event?" asked Tony. "How about a mud-wrestling contest. Krunchensnap vs. Pimple-head Charlie. Once we catch him..."

"If your father ever catches that scoundrel, there won't be enough left of him to wrestle anybody," she said.

An idea popped into my head. We should tell her that we saw Charlie in the girls' bathroom. But then we'd have to explain about the so-called "manure cigars" and being sent to the principal's office, and it just sounded too complicated. I let the thought whiz back out into the cosmos. Later...maybe.

Mrs. Ragusa picked up her purse and walked toward the side door. "Lasagna's in the oven, salad's in the refrigerator, and after the little ones are in bed, there are six different flavors of ice cream in the freezer. We're meeting at Max's house, so you know the number."

"I do," I said. "I hope she's finished vacuuming."

"Shut up," said Max.

After dinner, we played with the little Ragusas until they tired us out. We put them to bed and cleaned up the kitchen. We were polishing off the last of the ice cream when Mrs. Ragusa came back. She flopped into a kitchen chair and tossed her purse onto the table.

"We still don't know what we're going to do!" She

sighed. "How did everything go? Okay?"

Tony nodded. "No problem."

"Thank you," said Mrs. Ragusa. "You did a nice job cleaning up. It's getting late and, as much as I hate to remind you, there's school tomorrow. I'll clean up what's left. Don't forget to brush your teeth."

My mother always said the same thing. I had this vision of me being old and my poor ancient mother in bed surrounded by candles. The doctor is muttering, "No hope, no hope." Then, just as her spirit starts to rise toward heaven, Mom reaches out toward me and says, "Don't forget to brush your teeth."

We unrolled our sleeping bags in the living room and settled in for the night. Rosy was curled up at my feet.

Tony put a flashlight on the coffee table and said, "Just in case someone has to go wee-wee."

We talked for a while about Miss Butters. Even though we were worried about her, we didn't know what we could do about it. Was Pimple-head Charlie involved? According to Tony, Charlie had Angelina scrubbing pipes. Were Miss Butters and the newly missing custodian down the drain somewhere? More pipe scrubbers? How did Charlie get them down there? But more important, how were we going to get ourselves off Krunchensnap's manure list for the non-smoking incident? And then there was Daniela and Lindsey. They were also on the list and they hadn't even done anything. Not that we'd done anything, either. Was Krunchensnap really going to pin the theft of her trophy on us? Why would she do that? Was she that mean? What a dumb question!

I nodded off and woke to the sound of the Ragusa's old mantel clock striking three. Rosy was gone. There was a light on in the kitchen, the refrigerator light. Max was still sleeping, but Tony was wide awake. He shook Max gently. When Max started to say something, Tony covered his mouth and pointed toward the kitchen.

A thin shadow moved up the wall. "It's him," Tony whispered. He picked up the flashlight.

We crept to the open kitchen door and peeked around the corner.

There he was. I'm not kidding. In the flesh, Pimple-head Charlie! He was sitting at the kitchen table, eating. He was small and thin, his skin the color of lime-green Jell-O. You could almost see through his head. He wore an oversized shirt with a name stitched on its pocket. A glass of chocolate milk was next to his plate. He was humming softly to himself and doing the crossword puzzle in the newspaper.

Rosy was sitting next to him lapping up milk from a small bowl on the floor. Every now and then, Charlie would reach down without taking his eyes off the puzzle and scratch Rosy behind the ears.

Tony counted off silently on his raised fingers. Three, two, one! "NOW!"

Charlie jumped straight up from his chair as we rushed into the kitchen. My heart was pounding. Man, he was fast! He headed straight for the sink but Max was already there, covering the drain hole. Charlie panicked. He turned every way he could. His chest heaved, his eyes as big as saucers.

Rosy scampered into the living room.

I covered the heater register as Tony dived for Charlie. Charlie streaked past Tony and down the hall. The bathroom! He was headed for the bathroom! The door was closed and Tony was on top of him. Charlie squirted out from under him and headed for the only open door in the hall. He scooted into a bedroom, but we were right behind him.

Tony pulled the door closed. "Got him," he whispered. "There's no way out except through this door. Cover the vent."

"Whose room is this?" I whispered.

"Angelina's. Ready?"

We nodded and Tony turned on the light.

"Ohhh," moaned a weak voice from under the bed.

Max crawled over to one side of the bed and Tony crawled to the other, shining the flashlight.

"Ohhh, please, you're hurting my eyes! Turn it off."

"Come out of there!" Tony demanded.

"No! You'll hurt me! I wasn't doing anything wrong. Please, turn off the light."

"I don't trust you!" growled Tony. "Don't try anything funny!"

"Like what?"

"Like shoving someone down a drainpipe! I know my pipes."

I looked under the bed. "Sheesh. He's smaller than me. He doesn't look dangerous."

"You can be small and still be dangerous," announced Max. "The Irukandji jellyfish is barely a quarter-inch long and it's more deadly than a cobra."

I let out a puff of tired air. "Thank you, Max. Next time I see a jellyfish, I'll try not to let it get too close."

"Not only that, but the butterflyfish can—"

"Come out!" Tony interrupted. He turned off the flashlight. "Come out or I'll pull you out!"

Charlie poked his head out cautiously. He crawled to the other side of the room. "The light," he moaned, shielding his eyes.

I slid a small trunk over the heater register, turned on the desk lamp, and turned off the overhead light.

"Sit down," ordered Tony.

Charlie sat down at the desk, shaking. His thin legs dangled freely over the chair. He reminded me of a fish that my Great Aunt Henrietta used to keep in a tropical fish tank. It was called a glass catfish, and you could see all the guts and everything, even its bones. Charlie wasn't much different. There were bandages taped to the top of his bald head, his nose was sharp and now that the light was dim, his eyes seemed smaller and very black.

"I'd say you were about the 25th percentile on Dr. Meyers' growth chart," I said.

"Explain yourself!" Tony demanded

"What?"

"What are you doing in our house? What were you going to do, stuff one of my little brothers or sisters down the drain?"

"Oh," gasped Charlie. "What a horrid thing to say! I came for the lasagna. Next to the school cafeteria's, it's the absolute best!"

"Oh, right," said Tony sarcastically.

"What happened to your head?" Max asked.

Charlie rubbed the top of his bald dome. "Mrs. Ragusa turned on her new garbage disposal while I was coming up the drain."

"Listen, Charlie—"

"And stop calling me Charlie." He pointed to the name embroidered over the pocket of his oversized shirt. Below the words "Napa Auto Parts," it said "Lou."

"Where's my sister?" Tony demanded.

Suddenly the door flew open.

"What are you little twerps doing in my room?" Angelina Ragusa demanded. She stood in the doorway, tall and angry. In one hand was an old leather suitcase. The other hand was balled up into a fist that was firmly planted on her hip.

"You escaped?" asked Tony.

Angelina tossed the suitcase onto the bed. "What?"

"You know, Charlie," said Tony. "Down the drain."

"He's down the drain, all right," sneered Angelina. "I never want to set eyes on Charles A. Geetzbeet again! I don't care how much money his father has, he's still a jerk! Now get out of my room and take your weird little friend with you!"

But we couldn't. He was already gone.

9

The Bargain

Most of the following day was spent talking about Lou, formerly known as Pimple-head Charlie, and wondering if we should tell anyone about him. If he was taking food at night from the school, then maybe he liked collecting computers and big shiny objects like wrestling trophies as well? If he didn't take the trophy, maybe he saw who did. Maybe he knew what happened to Miss Butters.

At about five minutes to three, the classroom intercom crackled and Mrs. P said, "May I have your attention, please? This is a reminder from your principal, Ms. Krunchensnap, that the following students will report to the office promptly after school." She read off our names, followed by Lindsey's and Daniela's.

Butch and Slow Eddie snickered. They gave each

other high five's and went out the side door, laughing. We headed in the opposite direction.

While we sat in the office, waiting, Mrs. P looked us over.

I raised my hands in a gesture of helplessness.

"YOU MAY ENTER," blared the loudspeaker as the door hissed open.

Ms. K was sitting at her desk, wiping her nose with a damp handkerchief the size of a tablecloth. The door to her left was slightly open and I could see the corner of a sink but no gorilla—maybe Kong was at lunch. Her desk was clear except for the famous manure list. She folded her beefy fingers together as though she were getting ready to pray.

Lindsey fell to one knee and began to cry, begging for forgiveness.

"Get up!" Krunchensnap snarled. "I don't like crying. No one should cry, not even babies. Crying is a sign of weakness."

Daniela couldn't stand seeing her friend suffer. "But—"

"Silence!" Krunchensnap's eyes narrowed. "My spies are everywhere. I know exactly where you are every minute of the day." She blew her nose again. It sounded like the horn on a semi truck. When she was finished, she opened the handkerchief and checked the results. "It's these boys that I can't quite figure out. They're up to something. Plotting something."

Krunchensnap glared at the girls. "Guilt by association! I brought you in here so you could confess! Tell me everything you know. What are they plotting? They have a plan to overthrow the school board, don't they?" She pointed at Tony. "I heard that six years ago you stole the mayor's Buick and took it for a joy ride!"

"No, no," stammered Tony. "I was only in first grade."

"So what? I heard you were an active child. Big for your age. Precocious."

Time to turn on the humble machine. "Ms. Krunchensnap," I said in my most respectful voice. "Forgive me."

"HA!" she snorted. "You? That'll be the day when it snows in an oven, you little termite! I don't forgive. I get even!"

She raised the metal blinds a bit and peered out at the street. Parents were double-parked while they picked up their children. "Should be arrested for blocking traffic," she muttered. "Ha, forgive? Something has been going on in this school since I got here. Your former principal was too easy on you kids. He was a sissy. No wonder he lost his job. I can't quite put my finger on what's going on, but whatever it is, I don't like it. Kids nowadays get away with murder."

She stopped and blew her nose again. Her eyes squinted in my direction and she sneered. "Yes, murder. And what's worse, food is missing from the cafeteria, things are arranged differently overnight, weird noises are coming from the heater vents, and the pipes rattle where they never rattled before. Property is stolen, electronics, computers, and worse, my property, MY TROPHY!"

We could help with the missing food and the weird noises in the pipes, I thought, but I didn't dare say it. I changed the subject to the missing persons.

"Maybe we can help you find Miss Butters and Joe," I said.

"Find them?" said the Eye Popper. "What for? What's that got to do with my trophy? Wait a minute. Are you suggesting Miss Udders and Moe the custodian stole my beautiful trophy? Hmmm," she mumbled and looked out the window, smiling broadly when she saw a policeman giving a parent a ticket. "Yes," she said, "that makes perfect sense. They stole my valuable trophy, then ran off to sell it and split the profit!"

This was definitely taking a wrong turn. "I know you have a very hard job," I said in my meekest voice. "We'd like to do something nice for you—to try to make up for all the turmoil you believe we've caused in your life."

Daniela glared at me. "We?" she mouthed.

Ms. Krunchensnap turned away from the window and snorted. She reached down and pulled open a drawer in her desk and took out a large black box. "Did you say believe? You mean know, don't you, Mr. Boy Sprowt." She fingered her way through a thick section of infractions with my name at the top of half a dozen cards. "Where would you like me to start?" she asked.

I hung my head in shame. I should have been an actor. I tried to force a tear or two, but try as I might, I just couldn't muster one up.

She set the black box on her desk. "And what is it you think you can do for me?"

I said what I thought would matter most. "Maybe help you find the missing trophy?"

She slapped her hands on the desk so loudly and so

fast, we all jumped. Now everyone was staring at me.

Krunchensnap leaned across the desk. "What do you know about it? Maybe you and your gang of hooligans stole it. Trying to shift the blame on others? I wouldn't be a bit surprised. I'm onto your petty little scams! Harrumph!" She grunted, turning back to the window. "Won't work, Mr. Rusty Trout."

Rusty Trout? That was a new one. I looked at my silent friends and gestured wildly to please step in, I couldn't do this by myself. Help!

"The Torpedo," said Max, out of nowhere.

Krunchensnap straightened up, her eyeballs vibrated, her biceps quivered, and the veins in her neck bulged beet red. She turned and looked at each of us one by one and then stopped and glared at Max.

"What did you say?"

Max glanced around the room nervously.

We all stared at him. Where did this come from?

Max shrugged. "What? I just remembered reading about it in one of my mother's old *Crusher* magazines. It was on the wrestling channel, too. Big Mama the Eye Popper vs. Torpedo the Atomic Midget, two out of three falls. The Battle of the Century."

Silence.

"I don't know," he continued, "I just thought, maybe, if the Torpedo was still around she might have broken in and stolen it. Maybe she thinks it really belongs to her." Max shrugged again, sorry he'd opened his mouth.

"It doesn't belong to her. It's mine!" snarled Krunchensnap. She took out an old toothpick from a drawer, pried a wad of cafeteria taco from a molar, and flicked it toward the wastebasket.

She missed.

And then her face seemed to soften as if a distant memory surged through her brain. As if she heard the roar of the crowd, the cheers, and then, the agony of defeat. She sat down behind her desk and turned to look back out the window. The parents were gone, the streets empty except for an occasional car stopping at the stop sign. When a car slowed but didn't stop, she jotted down the license number.

She sighed.

"There were supposed to be three bouts. The winner of two out of three would keep the trophy forever, a declaration that the winner was the best in the world. That's me, of course—I lost the first bout because the Torpedo cheated, but I showed her. The second bout, I beat her fair and square, squashed her like a bug, the dirty cheater! And if the third bout hadn't been canceled because of the stupid storm that dumped three feet of snow that night, I'd have what I deserve—a championship, a chance to crush the Torpedo and show the world who was the real champion!"

Krunchensnap wasn't glaring at us any more. She had a strange look in her eyes, like she had sailed away on her own private sea of memory.

"What I wouldn't give for that third bout," she muttered. "What I wouldn't do to walk away a total winner."

Yes, I thought, what?

Max shrugged again. He was in a shrugging mood. Maybe he was going for a World Shrug record. He jumped back in. "If the Torpedo is still around, she could have done it!"

Tony and Big David nodded in agreement. Daniela looked peeved, tired of Lindsey clinging to her.

"What?" barked Krunchensnap. "I already know about the Torpedo. She retired, and to this town, too, so she is still around, but no one knows her true identity. The Torpedo was always masked. Besides, what's the point? Are you suggesting it was the Atomic Midget that broke into my office and stole my trophy? How do I know it wasn't one of you?"

"Because she has the strongest motive," I said. "If she didn't grab it herself, maybe she paid someone else to steal it for her...."

"Maybe she paid you."

There was a long pause. I looked past her and out the window. The broken glass had been replaced by a new pane, putty marks still smudged around the edges. And then, like a flash, I realized what it was that had bothered me so much about the custodian sweeping up the glass on the day of the break-in.

Krunchensnap tilted her head slightly and looked at me like a lizard waiting for an insect to crawl just a little closer. "I have an idea."

She sat down heavily and tapped on the black box, still staring at me with a strange, joyful wickedness that made me flinch. She picked up the manure list and put it in the box. "Now you and all your friends are in the box, there to stay until I decide how you should be punished for your sins. Unless, of course..."

We waited.

"Unless..."

"What?" Daniela blurted out. "Unless what?"

"Unless you perform one small task for me."

I had a sudden vision of the scene from *The Wizard of Oz* when the wizard made a similar request of Dorothy.

"What do you mean?" Tony asked. "Like what?"

"Like get my trophy back!"

"You want us to find your trophy and if we do, you'll tear up the manure list?" I asked.

Ms. Krunchensnap nodded, a lopsided grin on her face. "I knew you were smarter than you looked, Snoot."

"But we don't even know where to look," said Max.

"Simple." Krunchensnap rolled her huge shoulders and shrugged. "Start with the suspects, Miss What's-Her-Face, the janitor, What's-His-Name, one of you, of course, and the Torpedo."

"The Torpedo!" cried Max.

"Isn't that what the police are for?" Daniela asked.

"Of course, but children are everywhere. They visit each other, always sticking their noses in other people's business. Parents think they're cute, so they get away with things adults never could." She looked back at me.

"What is it, Mr. Sprowt? Something you'd like to share?"

"If we agree, you'll dump the manure list?" I asked again.

Krunchensnap nodded.

"No detention for David for whacking Slow Eddie?"

"Yes."

"Daniela and Lindsey go free?"

"Yes, yes."

"By when?"

"By the day of the Harvest Festival!"

Everyone started talking at once. "That's only a week away," said Tony. "How are we supposed to—"

Krunchensnap raised a beefy hand. "Silence!"

I put my hands behind my back so she couldn't see them shaking. "Okay, so if we get the trophy, you'll tear up the list, no letters to our parents, no accusations that we broke into your office, no suggestions that we were involved with any other stolen items from the school, suspension of any pending criminal charges, our good names restored to their former quality in our school community, and..." By now I was sweating, but decided I might as well go for broke, "and you'll dump the black box of all infractions by any students in the school!"

"You're pushing it, Sport!"

Everyone stared at me as if I had gone off my rocker.

Krunchensnap folded her thick arms across the desk and flexed her biceps. "Agreed."

She smiled as we moved toward the door. David tried to open it, but he couldn't. It was locked. We looked back at Krunchensnap.

"You don't like my company?" she sneered. "Anxious to get to your homework, like the good little students you pretend to be?"

Big David tried turning the doorknob again.

"In a hurry?"

She unfolded a sheet of paper that had been sitting on her desk under the black box.

"There is just one more thing. This is a letter from the International Mud Wrestling Association. It seems they have determined that since there was no third bout, the trophy should be returned to them a week from today. A trophy I no longer have. What to do, what to do?"

"That's the day of the Harvest Festival," said Max. "If we find it, are you going to give it back to them?"

"No. In your quest for the Holy Trophy, I want you to find out who the Atomic Midget is. I'm going to challenge her to the third bout at the Harvest Festival and beat the bejabbers out of her in front of the entire town. If she refuses, I will publicly brand her a coward and insist the IMWA let me keep my trophy."

"But that has nothing to do with us," said Daniela.

"No," moaned Max. "We only agreed to—"

Krunchensnap slammed her fist down on a red button and the door hissed open.

"Dismissed!"

10

The Iron Door

The next day dragged on and on. Somebody must have been fooling with the clocks again. Somewhere, some all-powerful being had picked up the universal remote and pushed the slo-mo button. By the time the three o'clock bell rang, we had become petrified wood.

I fell down in the hall on my backpack. "Can't move," I moaned. "Legs numb. Arms gone." I reached out to my friends who kept walking, more interested in getting something to eat than my welfare. "Hey," I called.

They stopped.

"We've got to find that dumb trophy," said Tony.

"And the Torpedo," Max added.

"I said what I said to get her off track. It seemed like a good idea at the time."

"Maybe," said Tony. "But it's too late now. The deal is done!"

I took a deep breath and groaned. "I know."

"How are we going to do this?" Big David asked. "We need some kind of plan."

"We should include Daniela and Lindsey," I said. "That is, if they'll speak to us."

"We could meet at my place," said Tony.

"Or right here," Big David added.

Max looked down the hall toward the office. "Here? What do you mean? Like at lunch? Recess? Where?"

Big David pointed at a door in the side hallway. "The custodian's room. No one uses it but Joe Asher and he's gone!" He opened the door a crack. "During the summer Little David and I helped Mr. Asher. Come on, I'll show you."

He reached in and turned on a light. We followed him down a narrow flight of creaky stairs to the furnace room with huge pipes leading out of the top of the old gas furnace. On one wall there were lockers and on the far wall there was an iron door. In between was a table littered with papers and stuff. More pipes of all sizes ran under the ceiling. I crossed the room and opened the iron door. It led to a crawl space under the main part of the building. A few feet in were two fresh mounds of dirt about six feet long. A rusty shovel with a broken handle lay near the door.

Kind of odd, I thought.

"This is perfect," said Tony. "This will be our war room."

"What do you mean?" asked Max.

"Big David's right. We need a plan." I said. "Miss Butters could help us. We need to find her. If we could find out who the Torpedo is, maybe she would come out of retirement and step into the ring with the Eye Popper. Maybe she already has the trophy!"

"That's a lot of maybes," said Max. "What if someone comes down here and finds us?"

Big David shook his head. "No one but the custodian ever comes down here."

We all sat down at the long table.

"Where's Lindsey and Daniela," asked Tony. "They're part of this."

"I texted them," said Max. He took out his phone and checked his messages. "Daniela said she'd meet us here."

"She said they'd come?" I asked, not believing they would. "Anyway, let's concentrate first on Miss Butters. We need to know where to start looking."

"How are we supposed to find her when the police haven't?" asked Max. "Where do we start?"

"Start with the facts," a tight little voice piped up.

We all jumped, knocking over our chairs. There was a clank of metal and then silence.

"Where'd that come from?" Tony whispered.

I pointed to the center of the cement floor. A six-inch drain cover lifted up, spun slowly across the room, and clattered to a stop.

We knelt on the cement floor and looked down the hole. Something blinked in the darkness. "Lou?" I called.

Tony picked up a broom that was leaning against the

table and dropped the long handle down the drain.

"OW!" cried Lou. "What was that for?"

"My sister," said Tony.

"Your sister?" said Max. "She ran off with her boy-friend. Plus she came home. And she treats you like dirt!"

"Yeah," said the voice from the drain. "Worse than dirt—sludge—and believe me, if you live down here, you become an expert on sludge!"

"Come up here," Max demanded. "I have some questions I want to ask you."

"No way!"

"How about if we promise no grabbing or whacking with broom handles or stuff like that?" I said, looking at Tony. Everyone nodded. We put our hands together and chorused, "Promise!"

"Where's the broom?" Lou asked.

Big David stuck the broom in a corner by the lockers.

"All clear," said Max. We sat down again.

"Turn the lights down," Lou ordered.

Max turned everything off except a small lamp that sat on the long table.

Lou stuck his head out of the drain hole and turned quickly to see if anything was behind him. He looked like some kind of bald prairie dog checking the terrain for chicken hawks. Slowly his shoulders came out, followed by his thin arms. He was wearing the same soggy shirt. He didn't come out any further. He rubbed his bald head. "That hurt," he said, glaring.

"Sorry," Tony mumbled.

"One more thing," Lou said, "and I mean this. You

can't tell anyone about me. No one. Not your parents, your teachers, and least of all, Krunchensnap. I'm taking a big chance by trusting you. I don't want to be put in a zoo just because I'm different. I like it up here. Where I come from, there is no day or night. It's cold, damp, and gray, gray, gray. I don't want to live down there anymore. Maybe we could help each other. Although I'm not so sure I want to help someone who drops broom handles on my head."

We all looked at Tony again.

Tony threw up his hands. "I'm really sorry, okay? You have to admit, he's kind of weird looking!"

"Extremely alien," agreed Max.

"Yeah, well," muttered Lou, sliding back down the drain, "if you guys were from another planet, it'd be the Planet Weirdo!"

"Wait," I cried. "Lou, don't go! You might be able to help us."

"Yes," said Big David. "Please."

Lou peeked out of the drain, waiting.

I spread my hands and raised my eyebrows in a what-do-you-think look. "He can help us. Don't you see, he can go where we can't. He could help us find Miss Butters, maybe even find the Eye Popper's stupid trophy. Find out who the Torpedo really is. Forget his looks and let's at least talk about the possibilities."

"I guess," said Tony.

"I have questions," Max said solemnly.

Big David reached out with his hand. "In or out?"

"In!" we all chorused and gave each other the secret handshake that bound our promises, our blood secrets, forever and ever, for all eternity, which meant, more or less, at least another twenty minutes.

Lou nervously scanned the room one more time and then pulled himself out of the drainpipe cautiously. He sat on the edge with his feet still in the hole.

"I love this room," he said. "Look at those pipes. And that gorgeous double cement sink." He inhaled deeply. "Smell that? Mold with a slight hint of dry rot. Lovely."

"The facts," said Tony.

"Oh, yes, well—"

"Wait, wait," said Max. "Let's clear the air here!"

Lou sniffed. "What's wrong with it?"

I was expecting someone to bring up my father's manure sacks, but they didn't.

"What I mean is, were you in my house? Was that you who knocked over those glasses while we were watching *Big Time Wrestling?*"

"Oh," said Lou. "I, well, I...yes. Your house has that wonderful wide screen TV. I love *Big Time Wrestling* and it's so convenient with that brushed aluminum sink against the rear wall. The door opens so easily."

"What door?"

"Not a door like you use. It's usually a drain cover or that little chrome plug at the bottom of a sink."

"Yeah, well," said Max indignantly. "Tickles got blamed for that one and I had to clean up the mess. My mother made me put him out for the night."

Lou rubbed the sore spot on his head. "I know. He told me. I apologized. I brought him a dead rat to make up for it."

"You can talk to animals?" asked Max, his voice rising. "What are you anyway?"

"What am I? I am what I am, just like you are what you are, no more and no less."

"Are there more of you?"

"No more of me," said Lou. "But, sure, there are others like me, just like there are more of you, except you're up and we're down."

"Hmmm," mumbled Max. "Upsiders and downsiders. Who would have thought?"

"Have you been in my grandma's house?" Big David asked.

"Just for leftovers. I like cold bone-warmer soup with a handful of asparagus trimmings."

Big David didn't seem upset about this new bit of information.

"Was that you in my house the night Annie got out of her crib?"

"She fell out! You don't know it, but she's falling out all the time. I'm always putting her back. That time she hurt herself and started to cry. I was making her laugh when your mother got up and you came tearing down the hall."

"Why didn't you wait and tell us?"

"So you can catch me and put me in a circus or a zoo? Forget it!"

I shrugged. "Dumb question."

Tony jumped in. "Remember the night that all this started? I swear I heard Angelina's voice in the heater pipes."

Lou slid down into the drainpipe.

"Shut up, you little twerp!" said a voice that sounded exactly like Angelina.

We looked at each other. Our mouths hung open, impressed with Lou's impersonation. I pointed at the hole in the floor. "Now there's a useful talent."

Lou came up and sat down at the edge of the drain again. He seemed much more relaxed. "Sorry I upset you," He said to Tony, a wide smile on his face. "I was just having fun. Like you guys do sometimes. Where I come from, there's no such thing as fun."

"There is one more thing," said Max. "One more question."

"What?"

"Why would you want to help us? I mean, what's in it for you?"

Lou pulled his legs out of the drain. He crossed them and leaned on his knees. "Well I..." he seemed to be searching for just the right words. I could tell by the frown on his face that this was an important moment for him. "I'm tired," he said. "I don't mean tired like sleepy. I mean tired of running, of hiding, of the sameness of being down there. There's no night, no day, and everyone looks exactly alike. We don't even have names. I didn't have a name until I found this shirt in the alley behind Brown's Auto Parts. I like being up here. I love the food. I love the school cafeteria food, especially day-old." He looked up at Max. "Your mother makes those great fried cookie things with the powered sugar. And you have that widescreen TV and Tickles and a family. There's none of that down below. Only shadows and pipes and big things that want to eat you."

"Big things?"

"Big things," Lou repeated. "Things that have been flushed away above ground and are still alive below ground. Some thrive, get bigger and hungrier, eat more and get bigger still."

Max went into question mode. "Like what? How big?"

Lou shuddered. "Crocs, goldfish, piranhas, rats, and, every now and then, hamsters."

"Just roaming around under us, down there?" Max asked, frantically pointing down the big drain hole.

Lou nodded.

"Mr. and Mrs. Wiggles," said Tony, staring down the hole.

"Who?" asked Max.

"Mr. and Mrs. Wiggles, my pet hamsters. Last year my little brother Benito took them out of their cage and tried to give them a bath in the toilet and accidentally flushed them away. I wonder if they're still alive."

Tony looked hopefully at Lou. "Small, cute, brown with white spots on their heads?"

Lou shook his head.

Tony sighed. "Benito cried for weeks. I didn't feel so good about it myself."

"I remember that," said Big David. "That's about the same time you got Rosy."

Tony nodded.

"That's another reason," said Lou. "I love that dog. And your mother's lasagna! And then, there's Annie."

"Annie?" I asked. "What about her?"

"She makes me laugh," said Lou. "And I make her laugh." He glanced up at the ceiling pipes for a few seconds and then let out the deepest, saddest sigh I'd ever heard. "I would never, never let any harm come to Annie! Never!" He shook his head slowly back and forth, his black eyes edged with tears. "Never! Never! Never!"

"What about Joe Asher, the custodian?" asked Max.

"And Miss Butters," added Tony. "Maybe you stuffed them down the drain!"

Lou threw up his hands. "The facts!" he said, standing up. He began pacing. He turned and faced us. "Look at me," he said. "The custodian weighs 300 pounds. Do I look like I could pick up a struggling 300-pound man and stuff him down a drain hole that's three inches wide?"

He had a point.

"And Miss Butters is no light-weight either."

Another point.

"Let's think about this," said Lou. He walked over to a locker and opened it. "Empty! It wasn't empty last week. The custodian used to sleep here when he wasn't home in his Winnebago. He kept a lot of clothes in there. Now, they're gone."

"So is the Winnebago," said Max. "I heard Mrs. Davis and Mr. Frazer, the seventh-grade teachers, talking about it. Someone went to the trailer court and the Winnebago was gone."

"Maybe they just ran off and joined the circus or something," I said. "I've thought about joining the circus lots of times. Usually during a math test."

Lou picked up a sandwich that was sitting on a pile

of letters. "Anybody going to eat this?"

"That thing's old," said Max. "It's got mold on it!"

Lou took a big bite. "Yum, Velveeta and bologna."

"I'm starting to feel sick," Tony muttered, looking out the small dirty window on the other side of the room.

"Wait a minute," I said. "How old is that sandwich?"

"Who cares?" asked Max.

"Lou, take a guess."

Lou opened the sandwich. "Hmmm, mayonnaise slightly rancid, bologna stiff at the edges, Velveeta cheese with small spots of mold, and lettuce completely wilted. I'd say three days, give or take thirty minutes."

"Wow," said Max, another expert on things no one else cared about.

"What does that prove?" asked Tony. "I don't get it."

Lou nodded. "I do!" He jumped off the table. "The facts. This sandwich was fresh on Monday at noon!"

"Exactly," I said. "The custodian was reported missing on Wednesday. But nobody can find him for days anyway. This was his Monday lunch."

"And he left in a hurry," said Big David.

"And that's the same day Miss Butters disappeared!"

"Shh," I said softly. "Someone's up there."

"Spies?"

I pointed toward the top of the stairs. "I heard something."

The door creaked open.

"Krunchensnap!"

11

Coffins In The Basement

But it wasn't the principal.

Daniela peeked through the partially opened door. "Psst," she hissed. "You guys down there?"

"Yeah, come down." I glanced at Lou. He looked like he was ready to dive back down the drain.

Slowly Daniela and Lindsey came down the creaky steps. When Lindsey got to the bottom, she looked around cautiously.

She saw Lou and her eyes went wide. "Snake!" she cried.

"Where?" Lou yelled. "I hate snakes!" He ran toward the drain hole. "Where, where?" he yelled again as he disappeared down the drain.

"That was the same thing we saw in the girls'

bathroom," said Daniela.

Lindsey hung on to Daniela. "Let's get out of here!"

"Just listen," I said, in my best parental voice. Surprise, surprise, they actually did listen. We told them everything, including how Lou could help us get off the manure list for good. They seemed a little calmer, but they were still skeptical, if not downright suspicious. Lindsey kept glancing at the stairs, ready to bolt for the door.

Daniela stared at the drain hole and then at me.

"This better not be another one of your weirdo jokes, Sprout!"

"Lou!" Big David called down the drain hole. "You there?"

"I hate snakes," Lou answered from somewhere deep within the pipe. "And what about those girls? Those are the same ones I saw when Russell was arrested by Krunchensnap for smelling like the back end of a horse."

"Jeeze," I said. "Can't we all just forget about that?"

"No problem," Daniela said, a tinge of suspicion still in her voice "Tell him to come up." Lindsey moved closer to the stairs, ready to run at any sign of danger.

"I'm not coming up unless you promise not to tell anyone about me. I don't want to end up in some carnival freak show!"

"Promise," Daniela called down the drain hole. "I give you my word and Lindsey's, too."

"I can speak for myself," said Lindsey, a trifle miffed. "I promise, thank you very much!"

"Okay," said Big David. "Come up."

Lou peeked out the drain, then slowly slipped out

and sat on the edge of it.

"Yuck!" said Lindsey. "It's a see-through salamander." She took out her cell phone. "I'm calling 911."

"No!" we all shouted at the same time.

"That's it!" said Lou. "I'm gone."

"Lindsey!" Daniela barked. "You just promised! Doesn't your word mean anything?"

"But he's really, really ugly," whined Lindsey. "And look how he dresses. Would you go to a party with a green newt that dresses like—"

"Stop!" Daniela hissed. "We all promised!"

"Okay, okay. You don't have to get all huffy."

Lou didn't say anything but leaned into the drain, ready to disappear.

Daniela glanced at her watch. "Can we get on with this? I have soccer practice in forty-five minutes and I still have plenty of questions."

"Of course you do," I said. "But first, I think we should check something out." I opened the iron door again. I pulled on a string and a light went on. It lit up the crawlspace under the building. "Look!"

Tony waved his hand toward the open door. "Two piles of dirt and a broken shovel. So what?"

"Hasn't it ever crossed your mind," I suggested, "that the Eye Popper might have smoked Joe and Miss Butters and then buried them in the basement?"

"No, it hasn't," said Max.

Daniela rolled her eyes. "You are such a weirdo, Russell."

"Haven't you ever watched *Blood on My Lips?*"

Lindsey cried. "I know what's under those piles of dirt! I saw it in episode six: *The Water Heater Murders.* The water heaters that were used as coffins. For once, Russell's right. Krunchensnap snuffed them and got rid of the bodies by stuffing them into the empty water heaters."

"Jeeze," Tony muttered. "One minute you're scared to walk into a basement and the next you're all excited about the prospect of dead bodies!"

Lindsey stared at the two mounds. She leaned toward the opening, a mixture of fear and joy in her eyes.

"Only one way to find out," said Big David. He grabbed the broken shovel and climbed in.

The space was colder than a morgue. We watched Big David shovel the loose dirt. Something white appeared, white and metallic.

"Hoyt 3000's!" said Tony.

"What?"

"Water heaters," said Tony. "Hoyt's a good brand."

"I knew it!" Lindsey whispered. "Coffins!" She hung on to Daniela's arm, squeezing so hard, Daniela cried out.

Lindsey shut her eyes and squeezed harder.

Big David worked the edge of the shovel along the rusty top. He wiggled the shovel back and forth until the tops popped off of both water heaters. Wiping his forehead, he held his breath and peeked into the tops of each of the heaters. After a second or two, he exhaled. "Pipes," he said. "The custodian must have put them here."

There was a collective sigh of relief. Except for Lindsey, who seemed disappointed and happy at the same time. Big David climbed out and I turned off the light and closed the door.

Silence.

Tony put his finger to his lips and then pointed at the small window high on the outside wall. Two shadows moved by and stopped. Someone rattled the window trying to open it. The outline of a face appeared, peering into the room. Butch the spy and his sidekick, Slow Eddie? But the windows were so dirty and the room so dim, they gave up and walked away.

"Anyone want any of this?" offered Lou, breaking the silence. A bowl of fruit spilled across the custodian's long table. He picked out a brown, spotted banana that was stuck to a piece of paper.

"Yuck," said Lindsey, sitting down at the big table. "You're not going to eat that, are you?"

Lou held out the sagging banana. "Want to share?" The paper fell into Lindsey's lap and a wad of brown banana stuck to her new white capris.

"Oh," she cried out. "Disgusting! Do you know how much these cost? Someone get it off!"

When Lou reached out to help, she jumped up and shouted. "Don't touch me, you two-legged jellyfish!"

"Hey," said Big David. "That wasn't very nice."

"I've been called worse," said Lou, eating the banana, peel and all.

"Yeah, who hasn't?" I chimed in.

Daniela lifted off the paper. She started to throw it into the wastebasket but stopped. "Look at this."

"What is it?

"I think it's..."

"What?"

"A love note." Daniela held the letter up to the light. She read it out loud. "'Yes, yes, yes, my darling Joe!'"

"From who?" asked Max.

"I don't know," said Daniela. "The rest of the note is too smeared to read. Here's another one. 'I count the minutes. Take me, my darling. Let us fly down the highway in the Winnebago of love. XXXOOO.'"

Tony leaned forward. "From?"

"I can't read it," said Daniela. "There's a pear stuck to this one. But there's a phone number written in pencil near the bottom edge."

I looked at the number. "Lindsey, call this number. See who it belongs to."

Lindsey gave a tired sigh, punched the buttons, and listened. "Oh," she said. "Oh my, oh my!"

"What?"

"It's the cemetery!"

More silence.

"What's this?" asked Tony. He reached across the pile of old fruit and picked up another piece of paper. Fruit flies rose up and he shook them off. A lump of what had been an apple was stuck to the middle. "It's to Joe," he said. "But the middle of the letter is gone. It's typed and it's from Krunchensnap."

"So?" asked Big David. "What's that prove?"

"Ohhh," said Lindsey. "Don't you see? Don't you ever watch TV?"

"No, actually, I don't," I reminded her.

"*I Love to Murder!*" said Lindsey. "Actual cases of murders committed in the name of love, jealousy, intrigue. Burials in the middle of the night, internet romances gone amok, interoffice arrangements destroying wonderful, solid marriages. Lovers discovered in cheap hotels and then buried under a new highway in Kansas."

We were all so taken back by Lindsey's sudden outburst, we didn't know what to say. She was on a roll.

"Krunchensnap!" she went on, "in a lovers' triangle with Miss Butters and Joe Asher. Don't you see? Don't you know what that spells?"

No one said a word.

"M-U-R-D-E-R!" she spelled out. "Murderrrrr!" Lindsey's eyes lit up like a strobe light. "And you know why?" She pointed at us. "You know what this is all about? Come on! Remember what we learned in fifth-grade Health Ed? That's what this is all about!"

We shook our heads. "What?"

"You know!" She winked.

"Anyone going to eat this apple?" Lou asked.

12
The Search Begins

We left school by separate doors to try to confuse Krunchensnap's spies. Lou stayed in the war room, but the way he got around, he could already be in one of our houses, making a sandwich.

Daniela rushed off to her soccer practice and Lindsey hurried home to throw her pants in the wash. Big David ran over to the portable to beg forgiveness for being late to his reading class.

Tony, Max, and I walked the few blocks up Main Street to the Model Bakery. Max had some money his dad had paid him for mowing the lawn and he offered to treat us to some of Mrs. Mitchell's baked goods. Sometimes when it was late in the day, Mrs. Mitchell would give us pastries that were about to become day-old. Sadly, she wasn't there, so Max had to pay up.

We sat outside in the late sun, chomping on Mrs. Mitchell's famous oatmeal cookies.

"We've got to find that trophy." I pointed to the hardware store across the street. "Steve's Hardware Store has trophies. Maybe someone tried to sell it there. Mr. Menegon and his brother own the place and they know everybody. Maybe they could help us."

We crossed the street and went into the store. Behind the front register were the trophy shelves. There were hundreds, but none of them looked like any of the trophies we'd seen in the Eye Popper's office.

"What can I do for you boys," asked Mr. Menegon. "Looking for a trophy? What's the event? Tony's dad buys all his plumbing supplies from us, so I can give you a great price. See anything you like?"

"Did anyone try to sell you a wrestling trophy?" Tony asked.

"Sell me a trophy? We only buy from dealers. Why? Is this for school?"

"Not exactly," said Max "We're looking for something much bigger than any of these. A mud wrestling trophy, a professional mud wrestling trophy."

"Someone broke into the principal's office and stole her biggest trophy," I explained.

"You mean Ms. Krunchensnap has trophies? Is she a collector?"

"She used to wrestle," said Max. "She was known as Big Mama the Eye Popper. I guess it was her favorite trophy."

"Wait a minute," Mr. Menegon cried. "Ms. Krunchensnap, the new principal, was Big Mama the Eye Popper?"

"Still is," I said.

"The trophy was for the Mud Wrestling Championship of the World," added Max. "She wrestled—"

"Torpedo the Atomic Midget!" shouted Mr. Menegon. "I was there!" Customers in the store stared at us.

"Wow!" said Mr. Menegon, shaking his head. "I'm a big wrestling fan and I never put two and two together. Big Mama is the principal, Ms. Krunchensnap? I didn't see the first bout, but it made headlines all over the country. I was in Chicago and saw the second match. It was the best mud wrestling I've ever seen. There was a huge electrical storm the night of the third bout. The whole city shut down. A snowstorm followed and nothing moved in Chicago for weeks. I don't think there ever was a third bout. Too bad, I'd pay plenty to see that! Any wrestling fan would! She was famous in her day. And no one ever found out the real identity of Torpedo the Atomic Midget."

"Ms. K wants a rematch," said Tony, "so she can beat the stuffing out of the Torpedo and keep the trophy!"

"When?"

"Saturday," announced Max, "at the Harvest Festival."

"I wish Miss Butters were still here," I said. "She would know what to do."

"What happened to Miss Butters?" Mr. Menegon asked.

"Gone," said Tony. "Disappeared."

"A week ago," Max added.

"She seemed fine when I saw her. Kind of in a hurry but not worried or anything."

"You saw her?" I asked. "When?"

"A few days ago. She bought a bunch of stuff in housewares."

"Was she alone?"

"I don't remember. I wasn't paying much attention."

Still here, I thought. "Was she—"

"We think the Torpedo lives in town," Tony interrupted. "If we can find her, we can find the trophy. We promised Krunchensnap an opportunity to win the trophy back in a rematch."

"Except we don't know how to find her or the trophy," said Max.

Mr. Menegon rubbed his hands together gleefully. "The Torpedo is here to challenge the Eye Popper for the world championship, right in our town! Oh boy! Wait until I tell everyone!" He rushed off, not giving us any help at all.

"Jeeze!" I said as we walked out of the store. "What's with you guys? I thought this was supposed to be a secret, just between us."

"How are we supposed to keep a secret and ask questions at the same time?" Max asked. "It wasn't like you didn't ask anything. I need information. I need answers!"

"Yeah," agreed Tony. "We found out something about Miss Butters. That could be useful."

"I guess so," I admitted. "It sounds like she's okay, but we need to find out where she is. And I still think you guys said too much. Rumors are going to be flying all over town. This is embarrassing, worse than embarrassing. This is out and out dangerous!"

"Jeeze, Sprout! Will you relax?" Tony rolled his eyes. He was good at it. When you got eye-rolled by Tony, you were supposed to feel demoted to moron level and be prepared to apologize for your stupidity.

Max patted me on my back. "Chill out, bud!"

"Yeah," said Tony. "Don't have a coronary trombone."

"A what?"

"Coronary trombone," repeated Tony. "You know. Like a heart attack."

"That's thrombosis, coronary thrombosis" I said. "Jeeze, I might as well be hanging out with Butch and Slow Eddie!"

Might as well, both of them were across the street, trying to look casual. Out of the corner of my eye, I watched them cross over and go into the hardware store once we were about halfway down the block. Now the rumors would really fly!

By the time I got home, my mother was setting the table and my dad was buried somewhere in the Sports Section. Annie sat in her high chair spooning up some beet and broccoli combo that was the color of stagnant algae.

"Ack!" she said and flipped a wad of it onto my T-shirt.

"Clean your shirt, sweetheart," my mother said sweetly. "Dinner's on the table." She hummed a little tune.

I put my backpack at the foot of the hall steps and

went to the sink. I washed my hands and then wiped the goo off of my shirt. Now there was a cold spot in the middle of my chest. "You're in a happy mood," I said. "Don't you want to know if I have a note from my teacher?"

"Do you?" asked my dad.

"No. I was just—"

"Haven't you heard?" my mother sang out. "My problems are solved. A wrestling match, a mud wrestling world championship! Isn't that an original idea? This will be the best fund-raiser, the best Harvest Festival ever! And your mother, sweetheart, is the chairperson!"

I felt like I was in Dr. Navone's office, our family dentist, and he had just given me a dozen shots of Novocain. I was paralyzed, speechless. An hour ago, Tony the bullhorn let the cat out of the bag and it turned into a rumor with an Apollo rocket strapped to its back. Except now it wasn't a rumor anymore. It was a fact.

The invisible man materialized, folded the newspaper, and set it next to his glass. "Your favorite," he said, pointing at my plate. "I picked up dinner from the Golden Harvest on the way home."

"What?"

"A double order of General Tso's Chicken."

"You took the general's chicken?" I said. "Won't he miss it?"

My father glanced at my mother. "What is he talking about?"

My mother reached over and felt my forehead. "Are you feeling all right?"

"Tired," I muttered.

"Why don't you go lie down for a few minutes," my father said. "You look a little pale."

Yes, pale...and tired, but not as pale as the general's chicken.

"Excuse me," I said, mournfully.

My mother smiled. "Don't forget to brush your teeth."

I went into my room and closed the door. I flopped onto the bed, stared at the ceiling, and tried to concentrate on what we knew. Anything? Yes, Mr. Menegon's news about seeing Miss Butters in the hardware store after she had supposedly disappeared, that was important. Mr. Menegon had said that she didn't seem any different. In fact she seemed quite happy. So maybe she was okay. Maybe she just took a week off. But where was she now? Something had happened, but what? And what about the custodian, Mr. Asher? Wait a minute, the glass, that was what bothered me. He swept up the broken glass from the outside. But if someone had broken in, the glass would have fallen into the office, not out of it. Which meant that if the doors were locked at night, then whoever stole the trophy had a key to the office, unlocked the door, took the trophy, and broke the glass from inside the office to make it look like a break in. Yes! Then they closed the door and locked it from the outside. But who had a key? Not many people—the custodian, Mrs. P, Krunchensnap. Anyone else?

Mrs. P, a thief? Hard to imagine. Mr. Asher, the custodian? What was his motive? Could Krunchensnap have stolen her own trophy? Again, why? Maybe she just wanted the publicity, to get her name in the paper. Maybe she was trying for the district superintendent's job. Maybe this was a way to force the Torpedo out of retirement, so she could keep the trophy and not give it back to the Mud Wrestling Association.

My head hurt. There were too many maybes.

The next thing I knew, my mother was taking off my shoes and pulling the covers over me. She kissed me on the forehead and closed the door softly.

But even with a mother's kiss, I still couldn't sleep.

13
Bingo

Sunday morning after church, I rushed over to Tony's. I thought I was early but everyone, including Lou, was already there. He had the look of a trendy second grader. He wore a floppy hat, short safari pants, high white socks with an athletic stripe, sunglasses, and his old shirt with the Lou label. He was splitting a candy bar with Lindsey. Whoa! Things sure had changed.

We sat down at the kitchen table where Tony had spread out some city maps.

"How are we going to do this?" Daniela asked.

I kept thinking about the phrase 'keep it simple.' "Okay," I said. "Here's what we know. Angelina was never kidnapped."

"Thank you," said Lou.

"We're not sure about Miss Butters or Mr. Asher."

Lou looked startled. "What?"

"Relax, Lou! We know you didn't stuff them down the drain. But, according to what we could read of the notes we found, there was some romantic stuff going on. Maybe between Miss Butters and Joe Asher, maybe not. Mr. Menegon said he saw Miss Butters a few days after she 'disappeared' and she seemed happy."

"So maybe she just took the week off," Big David suggested.

"And maybe the custodian dumped his clothes in the sink, changed, and drove off in his Winnebago to find greener pastures," Tony added.

Max tapped on the table. "There are a lot of unanswered questions here."

"It's so obvious," Lindsey remarked, waving her hand toward the ceiling. "Duh! Love notes, missing Winnebago, star crossed lovers. I saw the whole episode on that TV series about lumberjacks in love called *Splinters.*"

Daniela shook her head. "Maybe Miss Butters hasn't been kidnapped. She definitely wasn't stuffed down a drain. Lindsey, call Gretchen and ask her if she heard her father, Mr. Police Chief, say anything about a missing person report."

"Okay, okay!" Lindsey said, making the call. "Hi, Gretch. What are you doing? Oh, really, the sweater with the pink buttons on the sleeves? I love that. Guess who sent Byran a love note? Byran, you know, in Mrs. Davis's class, the cute one. No, no, no, but you're getting warmer. Oh, you're so close!"

"Lindsey!" we all shouted.

"What?"

Daniela raised her hands in exasperation. "Miss Butters!"

"Oh. I'm supposed to ask you if you heard anything about Miss Butters," she said, looking back at Daniela as though to say, "Are you happy now?"

"Oh, really? Why?"

"Ask her about Mr. Asher," I added.

Lindsey waved me away. "And what about the custodian? No kidding! You think? Me, too! Did you see the last episode of *Who Threw the Monkey Wrench into the Love Machine?* Oh, I know. No, that was the one where she beat him to death with the frozen ham. Oh, I know. Oh, I know."

Daniela snatched the phone away. "Thanks, Gretchen," she said and hung up.

"Hey! I wasn't finished!"

"So what about Miss Butters?" asked Max.

"Nothing. Same for Mr. Asher, I'm telling you. It's a secret love triangle, Krunchensnap, Miss Butters, and the custodian. Haven't you watched the new season of *Three's a Crowd?*"

"Can we get back to our own reality show here?" I asked. "What we know is that we're all on Krunchensnap's list. She hates me most of all. She'd do just about anything to see the last of me. But what's the one thing that she wants even more?"

"Her dumb trophy," Tony grumbled. He glanced over at Lou. "Other stuff has gone missing, too."

"What?" Lou cried. "Are you suggesting I'm a

thief? I may eat some school leftovers once in a while and rearrange the furniture a bit, but I'm no thief!"

"None of us stole anything," said Big David. "Can we get back to Russell's question?"

"Yeah," muttered Tony. "Sorry."

Lou shrugged.

"A rematch!" said Daniela. "That's what she wants most of all."

"Yes! We have to find out who the Torpedo is. Maybe she even has the trophy."

"Once it's found, the only way Ms. K can keep it would be to win the final bout with the Torpedo," reasoned Big David. "But we have no trophy, no Atomic Midget, no rematch."

"Somebody believes that bout is going to happen," said Max. "My dad said Central Valley Builders are bringing in a backhoe and lumber to build the wrestling arena in the middle of Carpy Field. It'll be finished by Friday. They're moving in bleachers, enough to seat a thousand people!"

I suddenly felt weak. A thousand people? "Okay," I said. "I have a plan. We know the Torpedo is someone who lives here. We know whoever it is has to be about the same build and the same age as Ms. K. Focus on the wrestler first, trophy second. Find the midget, and that's probably where the trophy will be."

Everyone groaned.

"There are five thousand people in this town," said Daniela.

"Yes," I said, "but not five thousand Atomic Midgets.

Not five thousand short middle-aged women who have muscles."

We all made separate lists of the people we thought fit the description of the Torpedo. We checked each other's lists and one by one, the lists got shorter and shorter. We used Tony's phone book and borrowed cell phones. We talked to Mrs. Russ at Main Street Books and Mrs. Stanton at the library to ask if anyone had bought or borrowed wrestling books lately. We called Mr. Wellington, the sports announcer at KGO TV. We called the radio station and Ms. Critchfield, the town historian. Most people were nice. Once in a while we got yelled at, but we kept right on going. We called and called. The day trudged on and the lists got shorter and shorter. Ms. Greene, the butcher, was the last call. She said she had never been to Chicago.

We threw up our hands.

"Most people aren't even home," said Lindsey "We are toast!"

Tony picked up a yardstick that was on his father's desk and whacked the city map that was on top of the table, ripping it a little.

"Oops!"

I leaned over and stuck my finger into the hole. "Nice going!"

"Hey! It was an accident. It was an old map anyway."

"Not that," I said. "Look at the hole. It marks Grace Church."

Max raised a quizzical eyebrow toward me. "So?"

Tony touched the hole in the map and nodded. "Hey! Grace Church. Mrs. Mac! She's about the same age, has only been here about a year, and looks like an ex-wrestler."

"And short!" I added. "It's possible."

"She may be only five feet tall," Tony said, "but she must weigh more than my Aunt Philomena. That's over 300 pounds!"

"So she's gained a little weight," said Max. He turned his laptop around and pointed at the screen. "I looked up the Torpedo and here's what she looked like the last time she wrestled."

Everyone gathered around the screen and stared at the black and white image of the masked face of the Torpedo the Atomic Midget.

Daniela threw up her hands. "What good is that? How are we supposed to know what she looks like if she's wearing a mask?"

"So out of style," added Lindsey.

While Lindsey was reviewing wrestling fashions, I opened the phone book and looked up the number of Grace Church, punching in the numbers on Daniela's phone. I had to do it twice, my hand was shaking so hard. A message machine answered.

"This is Grace Church," announced the recorded voice of Father Mac.

I hung up the phone.

"Now what?"

We all had the same idea at the same time. We stared at Lou.

"What?"

"You could do it," I said, "and no one would know but us."

"Do what?"

"Check out Mr. and Mrs. Mac's house to see if the trophy is there. If it is, she's the wrestler we're looking for."

Lou glanced down at his socks. "I don't know. You were mad at me for being in your houses uninvited. I'm..."

"Breaking and entering," interrupted Lindsey, the expert on crime.

"He's not breaking anything," explained Max. "He's just entering and then leaving."

"And you wouldn't be taking anything, either," I added. "We just need to know if the trophy is there."

Tony unrolled one of his father's city sewer maps and tapped on a spot somewhere in the middle. "See. Right on Kearney, left on Madrone, up Oak Street, and right on Spring. There! Their house is right next door to Grace Church. Piece of cake."

Lou took off his sunglasses and floppy hat. "Easy for you to say," he muttered and disappeared into the bathroom. There was a soft splash, some pipes rattled, and he was gone.

No one said a word. The minutes seemed like days. Was there hope? Then the pipes rattled again and Lou walked back into the room, leaving a trail of little puddles. He had a towel wrapped around himself.

"Well?"

Lou clung to the towel with one hand and raised the other. "Good news and not-so-good news."

"What's that mean?" Big David asked.

"Let's have the not-so-good news first," said Daniela.

"I'd rather have the good news and forget the bad news," Lindsey whined.

Lou shook his head and tightened up the towel. "No trophy. No one was home. I looked everywhere."

The room filled with a chorus of moans.

"Of course not!" I said. "What was I thinking? Mrs. Mac wouldn't have broken into Ms. Krunchensnap's office. She couldn't have."

"Why not?" asked Max.

"Because there was no break-in."

"What are you talking about?" said Daniela. "We were there. There was glass everywhere."

"No, not everywhere," I said. "It was outside the office. Remember? Mr. Asher was sweeping it up. If someone had really broken into the office from the outside, the glass would have been on the office floor. Whoever took the trophy had a key. They came in, broke the window from the inside to make it look a break-in, took the trophy, then locked the door and left."

"Whoa," said Big David. "Nice job, Mr. Detective!"

I didn't get to bask in my brainy observations for very long. Daniela, the biggest brain in the world, jumped right in and crushed me with her logic. "So it's someone who has a key."

"Must be," I agreed. "I can only think of three people, unless there's someone else we don't know about. Mrs. P, the secretary, Joe Asher, the custodian, Krunchensnap herself, or?"

"May we hear the good news now?" Lindsey demanded.

We turned and looked at Lou.

Lou took a deep breath and grinned. "Well, I didn't see the trophy, but I found half a dozen neatly pressed Torpedo the Atomic Midget costumes hanging in the back of Mrs. Mac's closet."

"Bingo!" I shouted. "Mrs. Mac is the Torpedo!"

14
Count Down

We walked into class five minutes early, a record for me. We had made a solemn vow that we would behave perfectly. Daniela made me promise twice.

Miss Sally was in her favorite spot at the back of the room. Her eyelids drooped and her skin was the color of Wonder Bread. I wondered if she had gone home at all. Maybe she was sitting in some potting soil and had taken root.

I started doodling on the back of my math paper. Mrs. Mac was the Torpedo. That crossed off one of three things on our to do list with five days to go. That was plenty of time to convince the Torpedo, a.k.a. Mrs. Mac, to come out of retirement and wrestle Big Mama the Eye Popper, a.k.a. Ms. B. Krunchensnap, for the World Mud Wrestling

Championship and possession of the missing trophy.

I drew them wrestling each other in the ring. How could we make that happen? Krunchensnap was ready to go, but Mrs. Mac was the problem. Okay, not the only problem, we still had to find the trophy. But how could we convince someone who used to be a big time wrestler to get back in the ring with an old adversary like the Eye Popper? If she wanted the world to know she was the Torpedo, wouldn't she have said so already?

At noon recess we sat in the cafeteria eating lunch. Tony and I went through our usual ritual of trading sandwiches. My mother always made peanut butter and jelly, and his mother always made bologna and cheese. We never asked our mothers to vary it up a bit. It was easier just to swap.

Max was doing most of the talking, asking question number four hundred billion squillon and seven when I spotted Ms. Krunchensnap behind the lunch counter. She stuck her finger into the hot chili, inspected it carefully and then licked her finger clean. She nodded at Mrs. Muñoz and began marching up and down the cafeteria aisles, inspecting each child's lunch as she passed. She looked like the warden in a prison movie. If someone wasn't eating, she would show them a picture she had laminated of some skeletons and then lecture them on a proper diet. When the kindergartners weren't looking, she'd swipe a cookie from their lunches.

Daniela and Lindsey sat down at our table with Gretchen and some other girls from the room across the hall.

I looked down the table at Daniela. "Heads up, the warden's coming."

Krunchensnap stopped and stared at Lindsey's lunch.

"You going to eat those Oreos?" she asked. Lindsey shook her head no and tried to smile as she handed the bag to the principal.

Ms. K glared at the table, her eyes laser beams burning a hole into each of our heads. Oreo crumbs rained down into Tony's bowl of chili.

"You're on my list, all of you. And none of you are getting off! Unless—" She rolled her shoulders, cracked her knuckles, and looked at me. "Unless, Spoot, unless you-know-what happens. You're lucky this isn't the old days when children weren't pampered like they are today."

As Mr. Rodriquez, the groundskeeper, walked by, the principal grabbed him around the neck. "In the old days I'd do this!" She put Mr. Rodriquez into a headlock. "Or this!" She dropped Mr. Rodriquez to the floor, threw her thick legs around his waist, and began to squeeze the living juices out of him.

"Ms. Krunchensnap, please," he gasped. "I'm sorry I didn't mow the lawns like I promised, but, with the custodian gone, I, I..." Mr. Rodriquez's handsome brown face was turning blue.

Ms. Krunchensnap jumped up and shook a thick finger at us. "I want my trophy back!" she roared and strode out of the cafeteria.

Mr. Rodriquez pulled himself up by the edge of the table, took a deep breath, and wobbled over to the serving line. The cafeteria ladies had seen the whole thing. Mrs. Muñoz gave a nasty look at Krunchensnap's backside and then smiled kindly at Mr. Rodriquez. She gave him an extra spoonful of chili.

After lunch, Big David, Max, Tony, and I stood at the edge of Carpy Field and watched the builders put up the wooden wrestling ring. The field was fenced off with yellow plastic construction tape to prevent kids from playing on the school playground. There were backhoes, small tractors, and flatbed trucks loaded with risers. Hoses snaked across the field and men were unloading big pieces of plywood. They were going in and out of the big Quonset hut at the edge of the school property where Mr. Rodriquez kept the heavy equipment for taking care of the school grounds.

"Rumors." I shook my head. "Doesn't anybody check to see if they're true?"

"They have," said Max. "Your mother said something to my mother who heard it from someone else's mother who heard it from someone else who knew it was true because the person who told them was there when so-and-so told them. All reliable people!"

"It's a fact now," agreed Big David.

We stood there watching the hustle and bustle of the volunteer workers. They had erected two tall posts near the entrance of the playground. A truck with a cherry picker on the back was parked underneath the posts. A man in a hard hat sat in the bucket, rising higher and higher. He pulled up a huge banner that read: Annual Harvest Festival, International Mud Wrestling Bout of the Century.

"Beautiful, isn't it?" said a voice from behind us. It

was Krunchensnap. We smiled weakly. "Just think, in a few days the trophy will be mine forever. I don't know how you boys did all this. I'm sure Mr. Sauerkraut here was at the epicenter of this little earthquake, always full of surprises, full of secrets. I have a few secrets myself, a few surprises. In fact I have one for you, Mr. Russell."

Whatever it was, she wasn't letting it loose. Not yet. She was savoring it, letting it simmer, enjoying my anxious speculation of the future. "Just a few more days and I'll have my trophy back, for keeps!"

She looked down at us and grinned. "And if the Torpedo fails to show up, I'll still have the consolation prize." She tilted her head slightly. "I'll have you, Russell Stinkweed."

The bell rang and we walked back to the classroom.

"Well!" said Tony. "Am I the only one with that warm fuzzy feeling?"

The afternoon dragged on and on. What was with Krunchensnap? Did it ever occur to her she might lose the bout? I felt like I was trying to row a boat across the Sahara Desert. I got up to get a drink.

I turned on the drinking fountain and sucked up about a gallon of water. "Hey!" whispered a thin little voice. "I'm getting soaked here." I looked into the sink. An eye looked back.

"Lou," I said softly. "What are you doing down there?"

"Waiting for you guys," he said. "I have an idea. Meet me in the war room at three." The eye disappeared.

I told everyone about Lou's request for a three

o'clock meeting. When the dismissal bell rang, we went our separate ways. Butch and Slow Eddie were watching us every minute. We managed to shake them and meet up in the war room.

We sat at the table, waiting for Lou. Krunchensnap's voice suddenly rang out from one of the dark corners of the room. We jumped. Where was she? "So! This is where you've been hiding. Using school property in a subversive manner is a felony! You'll go to federal prison." A shadow moved and there was a deep, evil laugh. "No one gets away from the Eye Popper! NO ONE!"

Lindsey started to cry. We all felt like crying. We were doomed. Done. Finished.

Lou stepped out of the shadows, laughing.

We jumped up at the same time and tried to stuff him back down the drain.

"Wait!" he shouted. "Wait! Don't you get it?"

We didn't.

"Krunchensnap's voice" exclaimed Lou. "What if the Torpedo heard the voice of Big Mama the Eye Popper in her dreams, a challenge, an ultimatum, a gauntlet cast in the darkness of a sleepless night?"

"Whoa! What a great idea," I said. "That might be enough to get her into the ring."

"Why not just ask her?" suggested Daniela.

Max shook his head. "*Crusher* magazine said she got married and vowed never to wrestle again."

Lindsey rolled her eyes and looked at her watch.

"What about Krunchensnap?" Tony asked. "How do we know she didn't steal her own trophy just to make all this happen? Or to avoid giving it back to the Wrestling Association. She has a key to her office."

"There's only one way to find out," said Max, glancing at Lou.

"What? You want me to go into her house and look? Are you crazy? It's one thing to slip into a priest's house when no one's home and quite another to slip into the house of Big Mama the Eye Popper."

"Do it while she's at school," suggested Daniela.

"Were running out of time," I cried.

"Just go in at night and take a peek," Tony begged. "A quick glance around the place. She'll probably be asleep."

Lou tilted his head toward Tony and raised a thin eyebrow. "Probably?"

"Not even for a big dish of my mom's lasagna with garlic bread and Caesar salad?" offered Tony.

"And sugared Danish lace cookies for dessert?" Max sweetened the deal.

"Okay," muttered Lou. "But you're going to help me. All of you! Together! Tonight! I'm not facing the Eye Popper alone."

15
Shadows

The last bit of light cast by the setting sun splashed across the window, spotlighting the sweating hulk of Ms. Krunchensnap as she finished the final set of 1500 crunches. She liked to do three sets at the end of the day. She lay back on the mat, catching her breath, gazing up at the ceiling, lost in thoughts of the past week.

It had been a good week, a great week even, watching Sprout and his pals squirming and scurrying about, doing her bidding. Children made great slaves. Too bad you had to go through all this to get them to behave. Why couldn't they all be little toadies like Percy Johnson, or Butch, as they called him. Or like his buddy, what was his name, Edward? It was the parents' fault, of course, always giving in to their little angels complaining about this and whining about that!

The teachers were just as bad, defending the little imps that took up so much space in the school, muttering about too many meetings, too much paper work. Why didn't they just shut up and do what they were told? Who knew better anyway, the teachers or the principal? Would they dare to jump into the ring with Big Mama, two out of three falls? Not likely!

What was that noise? Was someone spying on her? Krunchensnap opened the window and looked out.

"Who's there?" she shouted. Shadows moved near the edge of the garage. There was a whimpering sound that sounded a lot like what's-her-name, the doctor's kid. What a crybaby, a spoiled rotten brat. They were all spoiled rotten.

A pair of teenagers walked by, laughing as they glanced at Krunchensnap who glared back from the window. "Spoiled rotten!" she shouted at them and slammed the window closed.

"Spoiled rotten," she muttered again. She did 300 250-pound squats and a 150 lifts with the 430-pound barbells, followed by 1,000 one arm push-ups. As she huffed and puffed, the image of the Torpedo reappeared in her head, along with the sounds of a screaming crowd of fans chanting the Torpedo's name. "Yes, well I took care of that on the second bout, didn't I? And who were they cheering for then? That's right, me, Big Mama the Eye Popper!" A faint smile settled on Krunchensnap's hardened face as she polished off another 100 squats with the 500-pound barbell.

She took a cold shower, slipped on her black robe

with the Gold's Gym logo on the back, and put on her slippers. "Nothing like a good sweat before dinner," she muttered. "Now for a nice char-burned steak and a gallon of Cherry Garcia ice cream. Fruit is good for you."

She set the alarm clock. "Early to dinner, early to bed, and up with the sun. That's my motto!" The last thing she liked to see before she turned out the light was her favorite trophy. But the table was empty, the trophy gone. She should never have brought it to school. Someone had it, someone close by, probably one of those kids, probably the ringleader, Master Sprowt, mastermind and plotter of subversive acts.

The pipes rattled under the old house and the sink made strange burpy noises.

Was there someone in the house? She looked under the bed. No one. The bathroom? Something moved in the shadows, something small, about the size of…no, could it be the Atomic Midget?

"I know it's you, Torpedo!" she shouted. She flicked on the light as the bathroom door swung closed. "I know you're in there! You came to steal my trophy, didn't you? Well, you're too late! Some low life thief already stole it. Where have you been? I hope you've been doing your crunches because I'm going to crunch you good at the Harvest Festival!"

Krunchensnap picked up a yardstick that was leaning next to a small desk. She threw the door open and swung the yardstick like a saber. It swished through the air. Nothing. The bathroom was empty. She stood there for a moment, looking at a puddle of water on the floor. Strange.

The shower curtain moved and she leaped forward, whacking it! The curtain crumpled to the floor, revealing a small open window that let in a cool night breeze. She looked out the window. Something moved in the darkness. "Who's out there?" she shouted. The window was too small even for the Atomic Midget, but she locked it anyway.

The grandfather clock in the living room struck the hour. It was quiet, not a sound. Or was there? She waited.

There, that noise again, pipes rattling, gurgling noises, the other bathroom, near the kitchen. Someone was in her house.

Krunchensnap tossed the yardstick aside and reached over to pick up the phone on the nightstand. She pushed a red button. "Home invasion!" she whispered. "2021 Olive Street. Send a couple of squad cars." Just as she was about to hang up, she had a second thought. "And send an ambulance," she added. "Someone's going to need it and it won't be me!"

She lifted a 200-pound barbell from the weight rack. Moving from room to room in sumo commando style, she stopped for a moment, swung the barbell from side to side and then moved forward again. What was that noise? Cupboard doors opening and closing? Was the Torpedo there, searching for the trophy? No one invaded the home of B. Krunchensnap and got away with it! No one stepped into the ring with Big Mama the Eye Popper and lived to brag about it!

Except the Torpedo! There, near the sink, a shadow in front of the open cupboard.

Krunchensnap filled the doorway. "A worthy adversary," she hissed. "But one that I shall crush. The doors are locked. There is no escape!"

"Oh!" the shadow gasped, backing up against the kitchen door.

"Cornered," sneered Krunchensnap. "Cornered like a rat." She raised the barbell over her head.

The quivering shadow reached behind its back and undid the back door latch. Suddenly, the door was thrown open. The specter launched off the back porch and crashed into a group of shadows, all shouting and yelling and falling over each other in panic.

Sirens wailed down the street.

Krunchensnap ran out the door. "Come back and fight like a man!" She skidded to a stop. Where was the Torpedo? There were so many. Torpedo spies? "Can't take me on by yourself anymore?" she shouted into the dark. "Too old? Out of shape?" She poked the barbell under a picnic table and a black cat yowled and shot across the yard. "You can't get away from me, you little weasels! I see you and your gang hiding behind my car. The police are coming. You're trapped!"

"Take this!" she yelled and heaved the barbell high into the air like a 200-pound steel javelin. It arced end over end and crashed into the roof of her Volkswagen.

16
Underground

We all saw it coming at the same time and dodged out of the way, trying not to fall over each other in our panic. The barbell came down on one end and plunged into the roof of Krunchensnap's car with a loud metallic crunch.

A police car skidded around the corner, siren blaring, lights flashing.

We ducked into the shadows of a hedge that lined the sidewalk in front of Krunchensnap's house and held onto each other. Leaves rained down as our dear principal beat on the hedge with a garden rake.

Another police car stopped in the middle of the street, its red lights bouncing off the windows of the houses. An ambulance pulled up to the curb, backing up with that weird beep, beep, beep, warning sound that lets the public know they're about to get run over. Up and down the street, Krunchensnap's neighbors stepped out onto their porches or peeked out from behind parted curtains to see what was going on.

"I surrender!" Lindsey cried out. "I love you, Ms. Krunch…"

"Shut up!" hissed Daniela. She covered Lindsey's mouth and held onto her tightly.

A neighbor standing on the sidewalk saw us. "Hey, you!" he shouted, walking toward us. "What are you doing there?"

We were trapped.

"Psst! Over here!" A grate had been pulled aside and Lou crouched near the opening, waving frantically. "Come on! Go on down. Hurry up!"

The neighbor ran toward us. "Stop!" he shouted. "They're over here! Police!"

"Come on, come on," Lou urged.

It was the sewer or the cops. Max went down first, David followed, then Tony. Daniela pulled down a protesting Lindsey, and I was last, except for Lou who jumped in and pulled the grate cover over the hole.

It was dark, very, very dark, and cold and smelly and damp. The noises from the street above us were barely audible, but we could hear the neighbor talking to someone who sounded like Gretchen's dad, the police chief.

"It's okay," said Lou. "If we go down a little further, just another block or so, we can go up another ladder that opens onto Carpy Field."

It was so, so dark. We could hear faint voices and the

swish of cars passing above us and below us, faint echoes, clicking, dripping, and scurrying noises, along with the sound of thick water moving slowly past.

Suddenly, a light went on. Max, Mr. Practical, had brought a flashlight.

"How did you know we'd be stuck in a sewer and would need a flashlight?" I asked.

"I didn't know," said Max, casually letting the beam of light take stock of where we were standing. "I just grabbed it and stuck it in my backpack at the last minute."

He let the light play across the arched cement conduit. It was about twelve feet wide with narrow concrete sidewalks on either side. A slow stream of gray water flowed down the middle carrying the things people were not supposed to toss down the drain. Here and there something would break the surface of the water and disappear. "Be prepared, that's my motto," he added, shining the light down the long passage.

"At least someone's got a brain around here," said Lindsey. "This is all your fault, Russell Sprowt. You and your dumb ideas."

"It wasn't a dumb idea to begin with," said Big David, leaping to my defense.

"Well it is now," said Daniela. "Now that we're wanted by the police and Krunchensnap."

"We didn't go into her house," said Tony. "It was Lou."

"Oh!" said Lou. "Now it's my fault. You were the ones who talked me into this mess."

"Children, children, children," I said in my most

sincere teacher voice. "Can't we all just get along? Can't we all just work together for peace and—"

"Shhh," whispered Lou. "Turn off the light."

Something in Lou's voice made Max do as he was told.

"What?"

"Shhh, listen."

There was a scraping noise from somewhere faraway in the darkness.

"What's—"

"Shhh!"

Lou pushed past me and took a few silent steps away from us. He started making strange bubble-bursting burpy noises. Softly at first and then his voice changed pitch.

"Maybe he has indigestion," whispered Tony.

"Will you shut up?" groused Daniela.

There was silence for a moment and then from somewhere close by came more burpy noises, almost as though Lou was getting an answer to the burpy question he had asked.

"I thought so," whispered Lou. "We need to move on."

"The faster the better," said Lindsey. "I want out of here."

"It's only a few turns away," said Lou. "But better to leave the light off."

"Why?" demanded Lindsey. "I like it on."

"The light attracts things."

"Things?" echoed Max. "What kind of things?"

"Big things," warned Lou. "Come on. Stay close to

the wall and far from the water."

We followed Lou, sliding against the damp, slimy wall and trying to stay as far away from the water as possible. After a while our eyes became accustomed to the dark and we could see something coming to the surface and traveling alongside of us. We came to a slightly smaller tunnel that emptied into the one we were in and Lou stopped.

"This way. It's just up ahead."

"There's that noise again," said Big David.

It was a scraping sound, like claws on stone. But now it was closer and joined by heavy snorting.

"Can we speed this up?" I asked nervously.

There was a scuffling noise and Lindsey shouted, "NO! NO! NO!"

Max turned on the light. Lindsey was pulling on the top of her purse while a six foot goldfish sucked on its bottom.

Daniela held Lindsey around the waist, struggling to keep her from falling into the water. Big David banged on the fish's head with his fist and yelled at Lindsey to let go of the purse.

"It's Prada!" she cried.

The strap broke with a pop, and the fish slid back into the water with the purse in its mouth. Daniela and Big David pushed the angry Lindsey forward. Lou tried to quiet her down, pointing at the second passage.

"Turn off the light," he whispered. "Shhh!"

"Now what?" Lindsey hissed. "Something big and bad in the sewers, something worse than a giant orange piranha, something worse than losing a Prada purse? HA!

What could be—"

Lindsey stared past us, speechless. Her eyes were the size of ping pong balls. "That!" she said, pointing across the tunnel.

We all turned at the same time. "That" was huge! It had short thick arms with bony pinkish fingers ending in claws that waved wildly in the air. Its body was covered in long shaggy hair, dripping with green algae. It didn't seem to have a neck, only more hair and a heavy head with black pebbly eyes. It sniffed the rancid air, looking up and down the tunnel, and then let out a high-pitched moan.

From somewhere deep in the dark another squeal echoed toward us.

"What is it?" Max asked.

"I don't know," said Tony.

A second, even larger creature, stepped out of the tunnel and stood next to the first. It reared up on its short hind legs and looked at us, sniffing the air. It screeched, threw out its arms toward us, and plunged into the water.

"Run!" I shouted, always the decision maker.

"This way," urged Lou.

We ran down the narrow tunnel toward the light of a street grate.

"David, you go up first. You're the strongest," Lou directed. "This is the drain that opens onto Carpy Field. Hurry!"

Big David reached the shaft and scampered up the rusty ladder. He pushed against the grate.

"It's stuck," he said.

"Push!" we all shouted.

The creatures cried out again as they shuffled closer.

Max climbed the ladder and squeezed in next to David. Together they pushed and shoved and finally managed to slide the cover open a few inches. Mud dripped down.

The creatures screeched louder. They waddled nearer and nearer, their hairy arms outstretched towards us. Lindsey scrambled up the ladder, pulling on Max's pants and yelling at him to hurry up.

"I am," he yelled. "Stop! You're pulling off my pants."

"Together," said Big David. "Three, two, one, push!"

The grate reluctantly slid open and more mud poured in as Max and David scrambled out of the shaft and into the fresh evening air.

"Go! GO!" Tony shouted. "Here they come!"

Lindsey was out of the hole next, followed by Daniela, me, and then Lou. We could hear the caterwauling creatures below as Tony stuck his head out of the hole, the last of us to escape.

"They're coming up!" he shouted. "They're right behind me!"

I reached over to help Tony when suddenly he disappeared back down the shaft.

"Ahhh!" he cried. He popped up again and Daniela and I grabbed his shirt. Max and David each gripped an arm. The creatures wailed as they tugged on poor Tony's legs.

"PULL!" Lou screamed.

We pulled! A long minute ticked by until Tony finally fell out of the hole and onto the mud with the rest of us. Max and David quickly shoved the heavy iron grate back in place.

Lindsey jumped up and down on the grate, yelling, "Look at what you did to my favorite shirt, you greasy, hairy potato heads!"

Tony stretched out on his back, panting, gulping in as much fresh air as he could.

"You okay?" I asked.

Tony lifted his legs and pointed to his feet. "They got my shoes."

17

Love Me Or Leave Me

The next day at lunchtime, a small crowd of students stood around the school parking lot commenting on the barbell sticking out of the roof of the principal's car. Everyone had heard a slightly different rumor of how it had happened.

"That could be me right now," said Lou. He glared at Tony. "You owe me a lasagna dinner!"

"Yeah, well, it'll be a while before my mother does me any favors. She was furious that I lost my shoes. That's all she could talk about for hours. I don't think she even noticed the mud on my clothes."

"My mother made me take off all of my clothes in the garage and go straight to the shower," Lindsey complained. "It was so embarrassing! She went on and on about not staining her new white carpet. She didn't care how I got so dirty, just that the rug didn't! She kept saying how she hoped none of her friends in the Church Ladies' Aid Society had seen me. It was all your fault, Sprowt! I hope you got a good beating!"

"My folks weren't home." I smirked. "They went to the movies with Max's parents. I'm sorry to disappoint you."

Lindsey folded her arms and glared at me.

"Maybe we should tell the police we were there," Daniela said. "My parents trust me. They didn't ask me any questions at all. I don't like doing things they wouldn't approve of. Maybe we should tell them what we've been up to. Maybe they could even help."

There was a quick flurry of "I don't think so's."

"First let's go over what we know and then we can make some decisions. Remember, friends stick together," I said, giving my best pals my best smile.

Tony nodded. "Okay, okay. So if Mrs. Mac and the Big K don't have the trophy, who does?

"I think we should just give up," said Lindsey. "Let Russell take the consequences. It was his idea."

"Thank you," I said politely.

I waited patiently for someone to turn to me for advice. It never happened. Daniela jumped in instead.

"Two things," she said. "One, now that we know who the Torpedo is, we have to convince her to come out of hiding and challenge Big Mama for the trophy. And two, we have to find the trophy and get it to the Harvest Festival for the big bout."

I couldn't have said it better myself! "I think there

are only two possibilities for the theft," I said with all the authority I could muster.

Daniela raised an eyebrow. "And those are?"

"Mrs. P or Joe Asher."

"What?" said Tony. "Mrs. P?"

"She has a key."

Max shook his head. "Why?"

"Revenge," Daniela speculated. "Krunchensnap is a pretty nasty boss."

But we all came to the same conclusion. Big David summed it up for us.

"No way!"

"I don't think so either," admitted Daniela. "That only leaves Joe Asher, the custodian. Custodians have keys to every room in the school."

Lindsey smeared some pink lip balm across her mouth. "No good," she said, smacking her lips. "Something mysterious has befallen him and Miss Butters."

"Befallen?"

"You know like on—"

"I don't want to hear anymore about *I Love to Murder!*" I was tired of hearing about a TV program I'd never seen and didn't want to see.

"Excuse me, Mr. Rusty Spud!" Lindsey snorted. "I'm not talking about that old program. I'm talking about the new one, *Give Love A Chance*. It's a reality program about young women who marry ninety-year-old billionaires. It's on at ten every Thursday on the Nature Channel. Or is it the History Channel?"

I shook my head.

"I don't think there's any mystery," said Big David. "I saw Joe Asher's Winnebago parked in Miss Butters' driveway last night. She lives on Crane, right behind us. The lights were on in the house."

"What took you so long to tell us this?" yelled Max.

Big David shrugged.

Tony raised his hands. "That would explain a lot!"

The bell rang and we went back to the classroom, thinking about what those lights might mean. Were the runaways back? I decided we should go to Miss Butters' house after school and check it out.

When I told everyone my idea, they all jumped on the bandwagon with enthusiastic support.

"No way!" Lindsey protested. "I have more important things to do. I have a pedicure at 3:30. My toenails are mess."

"Can't," said Daniela. "Soccer practice."

"I promised to help my dad," said Tony. "Ragusa Plumbing is installing matching bidets, his and hers, for the Popovitch's newly remodeled bathroom."

Max shook his head. "Sorry, Russell. My mother is having the last school meeting before the Harvest Festival and she wants me to help clean the house."

"Vacuuming?" Tony asked. "Don't tell me you like to vacuum in the—"

"Shut up!" interrupted Max. "And the answer is no! So mind your own business!"

Big David glanced over at me and held up his hands in a gesture of support for his leader. "I'm game."

The bell rang, signaling the end of lunch hour.

Lou stood next to us, eating a peanut butter sand-wich he'd found somewhere in the back of the cafeteria. The cellophane was still on it.

"Are you going to convince the Torpedo to enter the bout against Big Mama?" I asked, a measure of hope in my little heart.

He tried to say something but the peanut butter seemed to have sealed his jaws closed. He nodded.

"I take that as a yes?"

He nodded again.

"When?"

"Ooooon."

"Noon?"

"Ooon."

"Soon?"

Another nod.

Close enough.

The rest of the afternoon was spent doing the same assignments we had finished the day before. I looked back at smiling Sally. She was looking mighty wan. I opened my desk, took out yesterday's lessons, changed the date, and set them neatly on the corner of my desk. Done! Who says school is hard?

After school, Big David and I walked to his house. Grandma David met us at the door, happy to see her boys and even happier to guide us to the kitchen table where a plate of warm cookies was waiting. She poured two glasses of chocolate milk and set them on the table.

Before she put the milk back, she looked around the corner and into the back bathroom. "Mr. Lou," she said.

"Do you want any chocolate milk and cookies?"

"Done in a minute," came the answer.

"Mr. Lou is so helpful. He's giving the dogs a bath. He's already dusted the whole house and swept the porch."

Mr. Lou? When had that happened?

Grandma rambled on as we sat and enjoyed her wonderful baking. She fussed with some fresh picked roses that lay in the sink. "I want you boys to take these over to the new Mrs. Asher," she said. "And tell them congratulations."

"The new Mrs. Asher?" Big David and I chorused.

"Yes, of course, Joe Asher and Miss Butters. I talked to her this morning when I was working in the garden. Which reminds me, can your ask your father to get me some more horse manure for my vegetables?"

"They got married?" I asked.

"Who? Your father?"

"No, Grandma," said Big David. "Mr. Asher and Miss Butters."

"I just said that. They eloped to Reno last week. Isn't that exciting?"

Big David and I looked at each other and smiled. That's why they had disappeared! Had Krunchensnap known this? Of course she had.

Lou stepped into the kitchen, wiping his thin hands on a towel. He was wearing one of Grandma David's aprons. Two freshly scrubbed dogs bounced around him as each tried to out-cute the other for his attention.

"Done," he announced. "That was fun." He nodded in our direction and sat down. He certainly was looking chipper for someone who was almost impaled by a 200-pound barbell. Grandma David poured him a glass of chocolate milk. "So," he asked, "what's new?"

18
The Ashers

Big David and I stood on our newly returned teacher's front porch, holding a bunch of roses from Grandma's garden.

"How are we going to do this?" I wondered out loud. "We can't just ask Mr. Asher if he stole Krunchensnap's trophy, can we?"

Big David rang the doorbell.

So much for any planning.

The door opened and there she was, our long-lost teacher. How I had missed that smile.

"You're there!" I said.

"And here! Come on in."

We walked into a small living room that was neat and comfortable. It had a friendly, welcome feeling. Pictures of Miss Butters' past classes hung on the walls next to family photos. One showed a much younger Miss Butters in tights, a sparkly top, and tap dance shoes. She was being held up over the heads of three gorillas.

When she saw me staring at the photograph, she laughed lightly and tapped on the glass. "Mabel Syrup and the Three Monkeys," she said. "My two brothers and a cousin in gorilla suits. Our act didn't last very long."

"Wow!" I said.

"Sit."

We sat.

"Are those flowers for me? They're beautiful."

"You and Mr. Asher," said Big David. "My grandma said to tell you congratulations."

"Your grandma is a sweetheart. Joe," she called. "Come see who's here."

"Just a sec." The custodian appeared in the kitchen doorway with a pipe wrench in one hand. "Oh, hi, boys. Just fixing a leak under the sink."

"He's so handy," said the new Mrs. Asher proudly.

"I'm almost done," Joe said and disappeared back into the kitchen.

Mrs. Asher followed Mr. Asher and came back with the roses in a vase. She set it on the piano next to a photograph of her and Joe smiling happily.

"So," she said brightly, "tell me everything that's happened at school since Joe and I have been gone. I hope you boys have been behaving yourselves!" She gave us a teasing grin.

"Well," I started to say.

Mrs. Asher tilted her head and raised an eyebrow. "Uh, oh, let's hear it."

And so, she did.

We didn't tell her anything about Lou because we'd promised, and I didn't think it right that we should tell anyone the true identity of the Torpedo. What was the matter with me? Must have been all that Sunday School.

"I don't know why there was so much confusion," she said. "Joe and I got permission to take a couple of weeks off from Mr. Gordo, the superintendent of the school district. Maybe he didn't tell Ms. Krunchensnap until after we left. He knew we were going to Reno to get married."

"Must have been the shoes in the sink," said Big David.

"We were in kind of hurry to get going!"

"Ms. K was probably distracted by the missing trophy," I said.

The sound of falling tools rumbled from the kitchen.

"You okay, Joe?" Mrs. Asher called.

No answer.

"That's all Ms. Krunchensnap can think about, getting her trophy back and the bout with the Torpedo," I went on. "Everyone is expecting to see the fight of the century this Saturday at the Harvest Festival."

"How can I help?" asked my favorite teacher.

"If we could find the trophy, we could present it at the Harvest Festival. That would help a lot," said Big David.

"I'm afraid I can't help you there," she said.

"I can," said Joe, standing in the doorway, looking pale and sad.

"What do you mean?" asked Mrs. Asher.

"I'm to blame," he said and flopped into a stuffed chair. "I'm so stupid, I can't believe it."

Mrs. Asher got up and sat on the arm of the chair next to her husband. "What do you mean?"

Joe rubbed his face and sighed. "I did it for you!"

"For me?"

"I was going to sell the trophy and use the money to buy you a diamond ring."

"But you gave me a ring, a beautiful ring, your grandmother's wedding band. I love it."

Joe put his head in his hands and sank deeper into the chair. "I was afraid if I asked you to marry me and offered you that small old band, you'd refuse."

"Never," she said. The new Mrs. Asher put her arm around her husband's shoulder.

"I'm so ashamed," said Joe.

"Why can't we just return it?" I suggested.

"To Krunchensnap?" Joe looked miserable.

"What's she going to do, fire you?" But of course, she could. And probably would.

"Too late," said Joe. "Starting Monday I'll be working for Gary Menegon at Steve's Hardware. I'm too embarrassed to go back to the school."

"Why can't we put the trophy back in secret so Ms. K will just find it there?" Big David suggested.

Joe shook his head. "I don't know where it is! I have to call Chief MacCormick and just turn myself in."

"But, Joe," said Mrs. Asher, "you said it was your fault the trophy was stolen."

"Yes, it is. But I didn't take it. I got cold feet. I realized how stupid it was after I broke the window. What kind of man would steal? What kind of example would I be to the kids I saw every day? I hated myself for even thinking about it. I was so afraid someone might see the broken glass and try to get in that I sat in my Winnebago all night guarding the office. So stupid!"

"So who took it?" Big David asked.

"I don't know. The only thing I do know is that nobody from the outside climbed into the principal's office through that window."

"But the trophy was gone in the morning," I said.

"Yes."

"And only you, Ms. K, and Mrs. P, have a key." I said. "There is no one else."

Joe looked away for a moment and then a small smile flitted across his face. "Of course!" he muttered. "Why didn't I think of that before?"

"What?" I said. "Someone else has a key?"

"Oh, yes," Joe declared. "They most certainly do!"

"Who?" David asked.

"I'll take care of it," said Joe. He took Mrs. Asher's hand. "This time, I'll do the right thing."

19
Daniel Webster

With the exception of Sundays, every evening at the Grace Church parish house was always the same. After cooking and serving dinner, Father Mac cleared the table, washed and dried the dishes, put them away, and then set the table for the morning's breakfast while Mrs. Mac worked on the Sunday sermon at the kitchen table.

"There," she said. "It's almost finished. I put in a couple of Bible verses that you need to shout out periodically to keep the back rows awake. I saw some nodders last Sunday. I also added some subtle reminders to cough up a few more dollars into the collection plate. From now on, I will be personally responsible for passing the plate around. If someone doesn't drop in something I approve of, I'm going to stand there and glare until they do! Last week someone dropped in a handful of metal washers and a bolt."

"Oh, my," said Father Mac, standing up. "Green tea or mint?"

Mrs. Mac closed her laptop, put it neatly away in a black carrying case, and set it down on the table. "I think green tea. Tonight's our movie night and I don't want to get too sleepy. What are we watching?"

Father Mac took the boiling teapot off the stove and poured hot water into two cups. "One of the greats, *The Devil and Daniel Webster.*"

"Oh, I love that movie. It's so instructive seeing how the prince of liars works his will on people. The devil is always disguised, but good old Daniel Webster recognizes him all the same!"

The Macs carried their hot tea into the living room and set the cups down next to their favorite chairs. Then they quickly changed into their pajamas, returned to the living room and sat in their matching his and hers Barcaloungers.

Father Mac spread a soft blanket across Mrs. Mac's lap. "Comfy, sweetheart?"

Mrs. Mac smiled, sighed, and relaxed.

Father Mac adjusted the volume with the remote, looked over at his wife for approval, and when it came with a nod, he sat back and sipped his tea. Life was good.

Before long his eyelids grew heavy, and soon he nodded off, snoring softly. Mrs. Mac lasted a little longer, almost to the end of the movie, before she, too, lost track of the devil playing tricks on Daniel. "You're a sly one, Old Scratch, you are, but I know you when I see you, no matter what you call yourself," she muttered and fell into a restless sleep.

Lou could hear the rattling snores from where he was hiding in the bathroom. He was nervous, reliving the last nightmare inside Krunchensnap's house. But he'd promised he would do this for his new friends. The question was how? How could he convince the Torpedo to come out of retirement? He thought of lying under the bed and disguising his voice as Big Mama Krunchensnap, but when he peeked into the bedroom, the Torpedo wasn't there.

He slipped into the bedroom and looked cautiously around. The snoring was coming from the living room. They must have fallen asleep in front of the television. The bedroom was lit by a small lamp sitting on a table wedged between a pair of twin beds. Nothing was unusual about the room except what he saw hanging in the open closet, partially hidden by other clothes, hanging exactly where he'd seen them the last time, the uniforms of Torpedo the Atomic Midget!

He pulled one off of the hanger and held it up in front of him. Hmmm, if she was half asleep and if he wore the uniform, would she see herself and be more sympathetic to her own shadow? Her twin?

Maybe. Just in case, he went back into the bathroom, took off his clothes, and laid them carefully on the floor, ready to jump back into them if he had to leave in a hurry. He wriggled into the uniform and pulled the mask over his head.

He checked himself in the bathroom mirror. A little loose, but not bad. Lou growled at the mirror like he had seen wrestlers do when he watched television over at Max's.

He tiptoed into the living room.

There she was, the old Torpedo, Mrs. Mac, snoring away. She didn't seem dangerous. Lou leaned over her and listened to her heavy snoring. Suddenly, she shuddered and an eye popped opened.

"What? You? Wait, are you me? No, the Torpedo is retired." Mrs. Mac rose up out of the Barcalounger like a killer shark rising toward the surface under a swimming seal.

Lou gasped and took a step backward.

She rolled her shoulders and cracked her knuckles. She could feel the energy creeping back into her sleepy, tired body. This was more like it. None of this Mrs. Mac stuff anymore, no more of this kowtowing to all the parishioners, to all the people who wanted favors. No, this was more like her old self, her real self, Torpedo the Atomic Midget!

"You can't fool me," she growled. "I know who you are. Big Mama sent you, didn't she, the sly old devil. Thinks she can fool me into getting all confused. Thought I was re-tired, thought I'd forgotten about the third and final bout of the century. Well, I haven't! The Harvest Festival, one bout for the trophy, my trophy, you little devil. I'll crush you just like I'm going crush the Eye Popper on Saturday!"

The Torpedo lunged toward Lou. He dodged away, ran into the bathroom, and disappeared.

Where was he? Hiding behind the toilet? The Tor-pedo grabbed the edge of the bowl and ripped it out of the floor, held it over her head for a moment, and then heaved it into the bathtub. Water spread across the floor and gathered around a pile of clothes. The Torpedo took a deep breath and stared at the clothes. "You can't fool me," she hissed. "You're still here somewhere. Even the devil wouldn't leave without his pants."

She stalked into the living room, looking under tables and behind chairs. "Where are you? I know you're here somewhere. Did you change shape?" She looked into the goldfish bowl. "No, too small!" There! Who was that sitting in that stuffed chair? Was that Daniel Webster? "Hey, you! Daniel!" she shouted.

Father Mac tried to shake the sleep from his head. "What, sweetheart? What's the matter? You look upset."

"Look at me, Daniel, if you really are Daniel. Look me in the eye and tell me the truth. Did you put that bolt in the collection plate last Sunday?"

"What? My darling, no, no, I'm not Daniel Webster. It's me, your husband."

The Torpedo stared at the figure in front of her. "I know who you are," she said in a low snarling voice. "You're right, you're not really Daniel Webster. I can tell. You can't fool me."

"Please, darling. You're still asleep. It's me, hubby baby."

"Hubby chubby," said the Torpedo, rolling her shoulders. "You can't fool the Torpedo. I know who you are. You're the devil pretending to be Daniel Webster." She crouched down and threw out her arms. She circled the fake Daniel Webster. "Come on, you sissy. Step into the arena and give it your best shot. Hear the crowd? That cheering is for the Torpedo! The booing is for you!"

"Booing?" said Father Mac. "Oh, my. Peaches, my

darling, wake up. You're still dreaming. Daniel Webster was a movie. I'm me, remember? Your husband whom you love with all your heart and promised long ago that once we were married you would never wrestle again, remember?"

The Torpedo froze. She stared at the figure in the Barcalounger. Could that be true? He didn't really look like Daniel Webster. No, he looked like someone else. Father Mac? No, it was another trick!

"You devil, you! You think just because you're wearing my husband's pajamas, I'll believe you're really him? Not on your life, bub!" The Torpedo spun into the air and came down in the middle of the Barcalounger. The chair sprang forward and launched the couple across the room. They bounced off the sofa and rolled onto the floor.

"Sweetheart!" Father Mac pleaded. "Wake up! You're sleep-wrestling again. No! Not the half nelson! Oh, OW! Not the triple leg twists! You promised!"

"If you won't leave freely, then I'll just have to squeeze the devil out of you!" she said. She squeezed and squeezed.

"Can't breathe," Father Mac gasped. In desperation he reached over, grabbed his cup of cold tea, and threw it in his wife's face.

"Arrrggghh!" she screamed. She stood up, cold tea dripping from her nose. "You'll pay for that!"

Father Mac sat up, panting as his wife climbed onto the fireplace mantel. "Oh, no," he whined. "Not that! Not the Flying Steamroller!"

The Torpedo spread her arms from side to side and leaned forward. "Crush the Eye Popper!" she yelled and leaped from the mantel.

Father Mac rolled out of the way as the Torpedo landed on the floor with a dull, heavy thud. After a few minutes of silence she groaned and rolled over. "Is the movie over?"

"Oh, thank the Lord," said Father Mac. "You're awake." He helped Mrs. Mac sit up.

"OW!"

"I thought I lost you this time," said Father Mac. "You were the Torpedo again. You tried to squeeze the devil to death and smash Big Mama the Eye Popper, all at the same time. I think you really want to go another round with Big Mama at the Harvest Festival. Do you?"

Mrs. Mac tried to stand up. "Oh, my," she said and sat back down on the floor. "No. I wouldn't even if I could!"

"Oh, sweetie pie," said Father Mac, "because of our marriage vows?"

"No," said Mrs. Mac, "because I think I broke something!"

20

Doomsday Morning

Friday morning the Ragusa Plumbing truck was parked in front of Grace Church. Mr. Ragusa and another plumber were carrying a new toilet into the little parish house next door. A new bathtub wrapped in heavy brown paper sat on the sidewalk.

Tony and I watched for a minute. When Mr. Ragusa came out, he saw us and waved. We waved back.

"What's that all about?" I asked.

"I don't know," said Tony. "Father Mac said something about shutting off the water and needing some new bathroom fixtures. They're putting in a new toilet this morning, aqua, a Koehler, wide rim."

Max saw us and crossed the street. "What's going on?"

"Koehler, extra wide seat," I explained. "Aqua."

"What?"

"Don't pay any attention to him," said Tony. "He's mocking the plumbing business. One day when his toilet clogs up and he needs Ragusa Plumbing to rescue him, he won't be in such a hurry to bad-mouth the industry!"

"Why?" I said. "A toilet plunger only costs $3.99."

"Yeah, well let me tell you something about profit margin in this business."

Big David crossed the street when he saw us waiting in front of the church.

"News!" he announced. "Big news! Lou snuck into Mrs. Mac's house last night and changed into the Torpedo's uniform!"

"No kidding!" said Tony.

"Why did he put on the Torpedo's clothes?" Max asked.

"He said she was sleeping and he thought he could convince her to wrestle by whispering in her ear. If she woke up and saw the Torpedo, she would think she was talking to herself. You know, like a dream."

I shook my head. "Whoa. That's a stretch!"

"So?" Max asked. "What happened?"

"It didn't quite work out. She shouted something about the devil, Daniel Webster, and the Eye Popper. Then she went after Lou. He left so fast, he's still wearing the Torpedo's uniform."

"Great."

"It is," said David. "The last thing she yelled was that she'd squash the Eye Popper at the Harvest Festival. I think our plan is working. There's going to be a bout!"

"If this is good," I muttered, "why do I have such a bad feeling?"

"Big David told me about Mr. Asher," said Max, conveniently changing the subject.

"And the new Mrs. Asher," added Tony.

"Yeah, well," I said. "We still need to find the trophy." I shifted my backpack and together we crossed Oak Street and stopped to watch the activity on the Carpy Field playground. The construction was almost finished. The smaller games and booths for the Harvest Festival lined the sidewalk just outside the field on Oak Street. We saw our mothers and a lot of other mothers putting the last touches on the Doomsday Project.

"Where should we look for the trophy?" Tony asked.

"Joe Asher said he'd help us with that. He thinks someone else had a key to the office," I said.

The bell rang and we sauntered into the main building.

We looked for Lou but didn't see him. I hoped he was either wearing something over the Torpedo's uniform or Grandma David had found some new clothes for him.

Ms. Krunchensnap stood in front of the classroom. Not a good sign.

Behind Krunchensnap, the blackboard was filled with assignments for hundreds of pages of work. She saw us staring at it all. She turned slightly toward the board and than looked back at us.

"Idle hands are the devil's workshop," she said with a grin. She cleared her throat, sucked a wad of something up her nose, and swallowed. The grin disappeared with the wad. "I have some good news and some bad news."

Lindsey raised her hand. "Can we have the good news first?"

Krunchensnap narrowed her eyes. "No, you may not. I make it a policy to always start with the bad news. Early this morning, the teacher from across the hall—"

"Ainsworth," said Daniela, "Mrs. Ainsworth."

Krunchensnap rolled her muscular shoulders and glared at Daniela. "When I need an assistant, I'll ask for one. As I was saying, Mrs. Worthless, the teacher from across the hall, came into the room to borrow something and noticed Miss Silly laying on the floor."

"Sally," corrected Daniela. "Her name was Miss Sally."

Ms. Krunchensnap rolled her eyes and waved Daniela away. "Sally, Silly, who cares? The point is she was taken away an hour ago. The school has not been notified of her condition yet. I believe she has passed on."

A collective gasp drifted out the open windows.

"And the good news?" someone asked.

"She passed on with a smile on her face."

Oh, goodie, I thought. Was it rude to die with a frown on your face?

"Mrs. Unworthy will be keeping an eye on you," she said and left the room.

We all started whispering when Krunchensnap reappeared in the doorway. "I expect quiet!" she barked. "And I expect everyone in this room to finish the assignments I have written on the front board and I mean everyone. Or else!"

There was a moment of silence as she paused to let the iron words 'or else' sink in, and then she disappeared again. Mrs. Ainsworth peeked in as we took out our textbooks for the academic deluge.

"Daniela," she said, "If the class needs something, come over to my room and tell me."

Daniela nodded. Mrs. Ainsworth left the door open, crossed the hall, and kept her own classroom door open as well.

Almost everyone got busy right away. For those with brains, the 'or else' factor was enough of an incentive to spur us on. For those like Butch and Slow Eddie, the time was spent firing off paper clips and spit wads. Slow Eddie was having great fun teasing Gretchen. Every time she'd start to write something, he'd reach over and shove her elbow so her pencil would skid across the paper and she'd have to start over.

"Stop!" she pleaded. "Please."

"Oh, my," whispered Slow Eddie. "You gonna cry?"

"Knock it off," said Daniela. "Leave her alone."

"Oooooh, you gonna rat on me to Worthless?"

Big David glanced over at Eddie. "Stuff it," he said.

"Hey, Butch, look who can talk? Dumbo the Elephant!"

Butch thought that was pretty clever and laughed.

Big David's eyes narrowed and he clenched his teeth as he leaned toward them.

Uh oh, I thought. He's ready to launch. I reached over and put my hand on his arm. "Forget it," I said. "I have a better idea."

"Better than pounding them into the ground?"

He had a point. I'd like to see it. Everyone in the room except Butch and his buddy would have paid to see it happen. But I didn't want him to get into trouble, so I said, "Yes, much better."

He seemed to accept that, and even though he was obviously disappointed, went back to work.

What exactly was my better idea? Well, I kept thinking there must be a better, faster way of cranking out all of this busy work. Krunchensnap was never going to correct it anyway. Henry Ford popped into my feverish, sizzling brain. That was it, an assembly line. I copied down the assignments on a sheet of paper and next to each, I wrote the name of the student I thought was best in that particular subject. Then I carefully tore each named assignment into a separate scrap of paper and stuck them into my jacket pocket.

At recess, I told the Big Six my plan.

"Isn't that cheating?" asked Lindsey.

"It's efficiency," I clarified. "Like Henry Ford's assembly line."

"Who?"

"You explain it to her," said Tony, gesturing toward Daniela.

"The trick is we exclude Slow Eddie and Butch from sharing our information," I continued. "By lunch time we should all be finished with our part of the project, then we simply have to copy each other's work and we're done."

"I still think it's cheating," said Lindsey. "I have a

reputation to protect."

Max let out an exasperated sigh. "What is the purpose of going to school?" he asked, looking directly at Lindsey.

"To learn stuff?" she said, not quite convinced.

"So when someone passes you their part of the project, you read it carefully, reinforce the facts by writing them on a separate piece of paper and putting your name on the top, thus showing the powers-that-be, that you, Lindsey Meyers, have now spent your school day usefully, productively, and have learned something that your father the doctor can be proud of."

"Oh," said Lindsey. "OH! I see!"

We split up and talked to the other students. They loved the idea and when we returned to class, they got right down to work. When Mrs. Ainsworth stuck her head in the door, she was quite pleased by all the ants diligently toiling away. She wasn't so happy when she noticed Butch and Slow Eddie's blank papers. She reminded them to stop talking and get some work done.

"We're doing our best," said Butch sincerely.

Slow Eddie nodded sadly in agreement.

When Mrs. Ainsworth turned her back and left the room. Slow Eddie passed gas and said, "Oops! Must have stepped on a toad!" Butch thought that was hilarious.

Luckily, the lunch bell rang.

21
Doomsday Afternoon

After lunch we went right back to work. By the time P.E. rolled around we were done, our papers stacked neatly on the corner of our desks, ready to be collected by the agency in charge.

Even I felt pretty good and I wasn't much of a P.E. fan. People kept running up to me on the field and telling me what a great idea the Henry Ford plan was. Someone even suggested it be presented to the school board. I wasn't so sure about that, but I enjoyed the compliments anyway.

When we returned to the room, Mrs. Ainsworth was waiting to tell us that Miss Sally was not dead. She described Miss Sally's condition as "recovering adequately." The long and the short of it, we later learned, was that Miss Sally was not as calm and collected as we thought. It seems she was so nervous at the beginning of the school day that she needed to polish off half of a bottle of Jim Beam Whiskey to get her day started, and at the end of the day she was so relieved, she polished off the rest to celebrate.

To each, their own, I always say. I was glad she was okay. I shouldn't have thought those things about her. I vowed that if she ever subbed again I'd have much kinder thoughts.

At ten to three, Mrs. Ainsworth collected our papers. "I'm impressed!" she said. "I'll have to find out how Miss Butters instilled such a strong work ethic in her class."

She stopped in front of Slow Eddie's desk. "Where are your assignments?" she asked.

"Right here!"

Mrs. Ainsworth turned the single piece of paper over. "This is it? "It took you all day to write your name on the paper?"

"It wasn't my fault," he said. "Those guys kept making loud noises and being all distracting. I couldn't concentrate. I tried my very bestest."

She picked up Butch's papers. The top sheet had three math problems that were finished, two of which were incorrect. "You, too? This is a whole day's work?"

"Everybody is always picking on me," Butch whined. "I worked hard!"

"Really?" she asked, collecting the rest of the papers. She put Butch's and Slow Eddie's papers in a separate pile, attached a note to them, and then added them to the stack. She handed the papers to Daniela to take to the principal.

"With pleasure," said Daniela, glancing over at

Butch and Slow Eddie.

I looked over at Big David and smiled.

He returned my smile with a very wide grin.

We got our stuff together and sat back down, waiting for the bell to ring. Daniela walked back in and gave a note to Mrs. Ainsworth who showed the note to Slow Eddie and Butch.

"The principal wishes to see you," she said. "Now."

They left, muttering to each other.

Mrs. Ainsworth crossed the hall, dismissed her class, and then returned to ours. This was turning out to be a great day.

The P.A. system interrupted my mental vacation. It was Mrs. P. "The following students please report to the principal's office promptly after school." She read off the names of the Big Six.

Maybe I was wrong.

Mrs. Ainsworth dismissed the class as the bell rang and the six of us trudged down the hall toward the green room.

Mrs. P was on the phone when we filed into the office. "Yes," she said. "They just walked in. No, Ms. Krunchensnap, they're not late. The bell just rang a few minutes ago. Yes, school is over at 3 o'clock. I don't know why classes don't go until ten o'clock at night, Ms. Krunchensnap. Yes, I'm sure if you were the district superintendent, things would be different." Mrs. P looked up at the ceiling. She held the phone at arm's length. "Yeah, right! That and your mother's mustache!" She brought the phone back to her ear. "What? No, Ms. Krunchensnap. I didn't say that! I think this is a bad connection. I'll call the phone company first thing on Monday. Yes, Ms. Krunchensnap, I'll send in the little felons."

Mrs. P hung up the phone and sighed. She laid her head on the desk, raised her arm, and pointed toward the door.

"You may enter!" thundered the voice from the speaker. We all pushed and shoved each other, trying not to be the first one into the room. Of course, my muscle-bound, athletic, tough-as-nails, Herculean body failed again. They shoved me into the room first.

Krunchensnap sat behind her desk. There were two other chairs in the room. We would have used them, but they were occupied. Butch was in one and Slow Eddie in the other.

Krunchensnap allowed a smile to settle on her face. "Tomorrow is the Harvest Festival. First we have the parade down Oak Street. Then the kiddy booths are opened, followed by the luncheon barbecues. It's all such a festive moneymaker. So much fun. OH!" she said, slapping her head. "I almost forgot the best part, the main event, the third and final bout for the Mud Wrestling Championship of the World. Incredible! How could this happen right here in our little town?" She looked into my sweaty little eyes. "Who would have thought that someone like you, Mr. Russell, short of stature, but tall and wide of mouth, could pull it off? Well, you're still on my list, because I don't think the Torpedo is going to show up. So I have another suggestion. We don't want the crowds to be disappointed. They're paying big money to see a wrestling bout. I've decided there

151

should be another bout, a preliminary bout, a student bout."
She looked over at Butch and Slow Eddie.

Slow Eddie and Butch wrestling? No, there was much more to this. Shut up and wait, I told myself.

"It would seem that Edward and Percy were unable to finish their assignments in class today because they were being picked on and there was too much talking in the room by disruptive students, such as yourselves."

"That's right," said Slow Eddie. "No matter how hard we tried, we was like left out in the wildness, like a weed in the wind."

Krunchensnap nodded. "Very poetic," she said, "Thank you, Edward."

"What!?" protested Daniela. "These two pinheads were—"

"Cease!" said Krunchensnap, raising her muscular fist. "Stop interrupting me. It's starting to become a habit with you and I don't like it! I don't know how the rest of the class was able to finish all the work I put on the board and yet two of my star students were unable to. I believe you, Mr. Russell, are at the bottom of all this. So I've decided to let good sportsmanship prevail and allow the two factions to battle it out in the ring, two out of three falls."

We all looked at each other, wondering where this was going.

"Percy has volunteered to be one of the contestants," she said. "Edward has agreed to help, too." She nodded in Slow Eddie's direction. Slow Eddie nodded back. "Edward will time the bout. Two out of three falls. He will be in charge of the bell. That's one side. Now we need a worthy opponent for Percy. A volunteer, of course."

"Me!" said Big David, stepping forward. "I'd be happy to be Percy's opponent. Don't you think that's a good idea, Percy?"

Butch looked at Krunchensnap, fear in his eyes. He shook his head.

"Thank you, David," she said. "But I'm afraid you've had too many private bouts of your own this year. You're disqualified."

Butch looked relieved.

Krunchensnap turned toward me. "Anyone else?"

"You can't force anyone to wrestle against their will," protested Daniela. "It's not fair!"

"You know," said Ms. Krunchensnap. "You're right. I do want to be fair. As principal of this school, it's my duty to be fair." She picked up a piece of paper from her desk. It was the manure list. "I'm afraid I had to add a few new charges to the list. Oh, none for you, Mr. Russell. You're such a nice boy. But your friends..." she sighed. "Too bad. I do want to be fair."

She picked up a yellow felt pen from her desk. "It would be so easy to cross out all of these names, except of course, we made a deal."

"The deal," I said, my voice shaking, "Was to give you an opportunity to get the trophy back. I said I would take the blame for everyone else if you took them off of the list."

"Did I agree to that?" she asked innocently.

Everyone but Butch and Slow Eddie nodded.

"Very well," she said. "She pretended to cross off

everyone's name but mine and then put it back on her desk. "Any volunteers?"

"Okay," said Tony. "Russell volunteers and we'll be his backup crew."

Krunchensnap beamed. "Terrific! I guess that does it then. One small bout I will enjoy immensely." She winked at Butch. "And then Big Mama returns to take on the Torpedo, assuming, of course, the Atomic Runt shows up! Yes, the Bout of the Century. One fall, winner take all! Dismissed!"

We walked back down the hall. I felt dizzy. What had just happened? I thought we had conquered this day. How could I feel ahead one minute and end up behind the next?

"It's okay," said Tony. "We're behind you all the way. Right, everyone?"

"Absolutely!" they all chimed together.

Easy for them to say!

"Once we have the trophy we're all set," said Tony.

"Yeah, well, I haven't heard anything from Joe Asher, so I wouldn't count on it!"

"Tomorrow the Torpedo will show up and you'll be off the hook," said Daniela.

Max patted me on the back. "We'll all be in your corner. I watch a lot of wrestling, I know all the tricks."

"I won't have to get dirty, will I?" Lindsey asked.

"Wear your old clothes," said Daniela.

"I don't have any old clothes."

Daniela threw up her hands. "Then wear a raincoat!"

"Okay, okay," said Lindsey. "You don't have to get all huffy!"

Tony put his arm around my shoulders. "Don't worry. We're there for you. We got it covered. What can go wrong? It can't get any worse."

Where had I heard that one before?

22
The Harvest Festival

The sun rose far too early for me on Saturday morning, but it was right on schedule for everyone else.

I dressed and went into the kitchen. I felt heavier this morning. My father was making pancakes and my mother was busy pumping Annie full of this week's special: shredded liver chunks and broccoli juice.

"Short stack coming up," the chef announced.

I pushed one of the pancakes around, took a small bite, and sighed.

"What's the matter, sweetheart?" my mother asked. "You didn't bring home another note from—"

"No, Ma." I shook my head.

She reached over and felt my forehead. "You're not feeling ill again, are you? I talked to Max's and Tony's mothers this morning. Your friends aren't feeling very well either. There must be something going around."

My father put some more pancakes on a platter and sat down. "This is going to be the best Harvest Festival ever," he said. "The Mud Wrestling Bout of the Century. Terrific idea. I heard a rumor from someone at the bank that there's going to be a preliminary bout with a couple of kids. What fun. Gee, I wish I were young again."

I wish you were, too, I thought. I wish you, or anyone else for that matter, were the one getting in the ring with Butch. I thought of telling my parents that it was me who was going to be in the ring with Butch the Meathead, but that thought was immediately followed by another—let sleeping dogs lie. If I mentioned this little tidbit, I'd have to explain the rest. No thanks. Avoid the napping dog.

"Wasn't it your idea?" my father asked.

"What?"

"Wasn't it your idea?" he asked again. "A couple of weeks ago, you said something about Ms. Krunchensnap coming out of retirement and wrestling the butcher or Mrs. Muñoz or someone."

"It was just a joke."

"Well, somebody thought it was a great idea. Ms. Krunchensnap has agreed. Someone else said they heard the Torpedo was already in town."

"We've made more money on the advance ticket sales than we did on the last five Harvest Festivals combined," my mother said proudly. She looked at me with that sincere look that only mothers have. "Sweetheart," she said, "I think you and your friends would feel a lot better about yourselves if you'd take a more active and positive role in school activities."

Right!

I helped my dad clean up the kitchen while my mother cleaned up Annie and dressed her in her holiday best.

We left the house early and walked to Oak Street to watch the parade. There weren't any cars because the police had blocked off the streets from Adams to Spring. Annie sat in her stroller, happily watching the pet parade go by. My mother and father were having a great time. Their friends all stopped to chat about the big day.

People dressed in costumes led their pets down the street. Even the pets were dressed up. There were dogs, cats, chickens, rabbits, mice, and even a stuffed ostrich on roller skates being pulled by some little kid. Big David and his brother walked by with Grandma David and waved. Lou was with them dressed in his usual droopy hat and big sunglasses, along with a new tan raincoat that was buttoned up and dragging on the ground.

All the stray dogs Grandma David had collected danced around Lou on their hind legs, dressed in clown costumes. A big cat walked with them and whenever one of the dogs started to wander off, the cat would trot over and hiss something personal to the dog and it immediately got back in line with the others.

"That looks like Tickles," I said.

"It is Tickles," Max said. "He's been staying at Grandma David's house for the last week. I think he's moved in."

We watched as two hamsters went by rolling themselves down the street in a clear plastic ball. It made me wonder if they were related to Mr. and Mrs. Wiggles, the hamsters Tony's little brother had flushed away.

Next came the high school float with this year's Harvest King and Queen, followed by the school band. More floats rolled by depicting the grape harvest. After them was a small float with a sign announcing: "Student Mud Wrestling Bout." Butch was in the float's fake wrestling arena, jumping up and down on a stuffed opponent.

"Ow!" I said.

Max looked at me. "Worried?"

"Nah," I said. "Piece of cake."

"Absolutely!"

Don't people know sarcasm when they hear it?

Next came the high school jazz chorus, followed by a group of primary kids dressed as bugs and playing recorders. The Main Event float rolled by on the back of a 1968 Ford flatbed truck. Krunchensnap was dressed in her old wrestling uniform. She flexed her muscles, posing and waving to the cheering crowd. A mannequin dressed in purple was stuffed upside down in a garbage can at the edge of the float. Only the legs were hanging out. A sign on the can said: The Torpedo, R.I.P. (Rest In Pieces).

The Kiwanis and Rotary Service Club floats followed and Popo the Clown came last, playing a giant kazoo. On his rear a sign said "The End."

"Come on," said Max. "Everyone's waiting for us."

My father handed me some money for the booth games and food. "Thanks," I said, "I'll see you later."

"We'll see you at the wrestling events," my mother said.

Oh, yeah.

23

The Masher, Killer of Fleas

Max and I played a few of the games, but I couldn't win anything to save my life. Max won at everything. "Must be my lucky day," he said.

We met Lindsey and Daniela at the Face Painting booth. "Look," said Lindsey. "I had roses painted on my cheeks. Pink to match my new blouse."

"Do they have a tattoo booth here," I asked. "I'd like to get a skull and crossbones tattooed on my forehead."

"Oh, wow," said Lindsey. "Cool."

"Yeah, you know," I continued, "to strike fear in Butch's heart."

"Oh, stop," said Daniela.

Tony and Big David walked up.

"Any news from Joe?" I asked.

David shook his head.

"Great."

Tony patted me on the back. "Are we ready?"

"We? The we is me, remember? My friend Tony volunteered me to be the human sacrifice for Krunchensnap."

"Oh, don't be so dramatic," said Daniela. "You know she wasn't going to let any of this go until you went into the ring with the Masher."

"Who?"

"Butch," said Tony. "That's what he's calling himself. Butch the Masher, Killer of Fleas."

"Terrific," I said. "You know what I'm going to be called? Chicken, the Flee-er from Friends, because I'm seriously thinking of changing my mind."

"You already have a name," said Tony. "Somebody gave it to the referee."

"What is it?"

"The Masked Flea."

"That's it!" I threw up my hands. "I'm off. Exiting stage left, or right, doesn't matter. Good-bye, so long, farewell, adieu. Parting is such sweet sorrow."

"Stop," said Daniela. "We won't let you down. We have a plan."

"Oh, goodie!"

We walked toward the arena. People filled the bleachers. "Has anyone considered letting me in on this little scam? I'm the one who's about to get pulverized."

"No," said Tony.

"Oh, good. Now I feel better."

We stood next to the wrestling ring. Butch wore the same uniform he'd worn on the float. Slow Eddie stood next to the bell that signaled the start and finish of each round. A large flag with Butch's name on it flew from the corner of the wrestling arena. A small flag flew from the opposite corner. An upside down flea was drawn in the center surrounded by a red circle with a line through it.

"You both have your own changing booths." Tony pointed at them. "And there's a hose next to each booth to wash off the mud." He held up a paper shopping bag. "Here's your uniform. Krunchensnap left it with the referee."

"Where is she?"

"Don't know," said Max.

"I don't see the Torpedo either. No Torpedo, no Joe, no trophy, and I'm about to get the stuffing beat out of me in front of half the county."

"Try to look on the bright side," said Lindsey.

"There's a bright side?"

"My dad's here," Lindsey said proudly. School superintendent Gordo asked him to be here, something about insurance. He'll be standing by, just in case."

"Just in case of what? Drowning in mud? Suffocation? Broken bones?"

"Stop," hushed Daniela. She handed me the paper bag.

My heart was pounding. I looked inside. "Oh, good! At least now I won't be humiliated by standing in the mud in front of millions in my shorts!" I dropped the bag and threw up my hands. "This is a bad idea."

"It's okay," said Big David. "I promise you. We

won't let you down."

The loudspeaker squealed and Max's dad, the local expert on wrestling and the master of ceremonies, welcomed everyone to the Harvest Festival. He was dressed in waders and a striped referee's shirt. There was a lengthy recap of past Harvest Festivals and twenty minutes spent thanking everyone for making this wonderful day possible.

I didn't hear my name mentioned.

The place was packed.

"And now," announced Max's dad, "the preliminary bout of the decade." The crowd applauded politely. "In this corner we have..." He paused to read a card that was handed to him. "We have Butch the Masher, Killer of Fleas." Cheers rose up from the crowd and Butch stomped around in the mud, waving to his fans. "And in this corner," our announcer continued, "we have..."

But there was no one in the other corner. I was still standing next to Max. "This is only a movie, this is only a movie," I kept repeating to myself.

"We have, I think, the Masked Flea!"

There was a mixture of laughter and applause.

"Come on," said Max. He pulled me by the arm toward the changing booth. Butch and his pals made chicken noises.

Max handed me the uniform. It was about three sizes too big. I put on the leotard and the pants and the flaming pink T-shirt. The head mask itched. Max threw the cape over my shoulders and we walked out toward the wrestling arena.

The crowd yelled and clapped and, I'm embarrassed

to admit, laughed.

"Will the combatants please step to the center of the ring?" asked the referee. Butch danced to the center, waving to the crowd. I slogged through the mud and stood there, feeling very much like my new given name, the Flea. I didn't hear anything Max's dad was saying. He pointed to my corner.

I sat down on the stool. "I've watched a lot of wrestling," said Max. "So follow my advice."

"Like?"

"Stay away from him!"

So much for the big plan!

Slow Eddie rang the bell.

Butch raced toward me, grabbed me by the waist, and threw me into the mud. He jumped on top of me and shoved my face down. The referee pulled Butch up and checked to see if I was still alive.

Just as he stepped back, Butch tackled me and we went down together. "Isn't this fun, Mr. Flea? I've been waiting to do this all year." He twisted my arm. I rolled out from under him and kicked him square in the knee. Man, that felt good.

Butch complained to the referee about good sportsmanship and then turned around and knocked me back into the mud. He grabbed my legs, swung me around, and let go. I slid through the mud and stopped at the edge of the ring. I pulled myself up by the ropes and looked out into the audience. Mr. and Mrs. Asher were sitting in the second row right behind my pals. The new Mrs. Asher smiled and waved while Butch dragged me back into the middle of the ring. He leaped into the air and fell on top of me, pinning me down. I couldn't move. I could barely breathe. The referee counted to three and pulled us both out of the mud. He held up Butch's arm.

"Winner of the first of two out of three falls: the Masher, Killer of Fleas!" The crowd cheered.

I crawled out of the ring. My muscles ached, my head hurt, and I could barely breathe with all that mud shoved up my nose. Max was waiting with a hose. He washed me off with freezing water. I wobbled back to the ring for the second round.

"At least this will be the last one," I said.

"No," said Max. "You're going to win this one."

I coughed and spit out something nasty. "Am I? I don't think so!"

The bell rang.

Butch danced around me. He lunged, then pulled back. He clucked like a chicken, darted forward, and shoved me backward into the mud. As soon as I got up, he knocked me down again. This went on for a couple of years. Then, just to show how great he was, he skipped around the ring with his arms folded. "Can't catch me," he jeered. "Come on, shrimpy! Come on Mr. Flea! Knock me down."

I hung on the ropes, waiting for the nightmare to be over. "I can't do it," I moaned.

"Yes, we can," said Max.

There was that "we" again. Why weren't "we" in the ring?

"Wait till he gets in the middle of the ring and then do exactly what I tell you to do."

"Run?"

Butch danced around making rude gestures and noises. The crowd loved it and roared with approval. He raised his hands in triumph.

"Wait, wait," yelled Max. He looked over at Tony. Tony nodded and gave the thumbs-up sign.

"Okay," said Max. "Jump him!"

"What? Are you crazy?"

"DO IT!" shouted Max.

I shot off the ropes and threw myself at Butch. He had the strangest look on his face. He stared, not at me, but at his feet. He was struggling to pull them out of the mud but they wouldn't budge. Just as I hit him, his feet came loose, and he fell backward into the mud.

"One, two, three," counted the referee. He pulled me out of the mud and held up my arm. "Winner of the second round, the Masked Flea!"

24
The Third Fall

Daniela and Max helped me walk back to the changing booth. I hurt all over. Max washed me down with the hose again. Man, that water was cold! I spit out about a pound of muck.

"What happened back there?" I asked. "Butch was frozen. He couldn't move."

"They built the arena in the center of the field," said Tony. "They built it over the central drain. Remember? The same drain we climbed out of the other night!"

"So?"

"That was Lou."

"Lou?"

"Yeah, he was waiting in the drain and when Butch stood over it, he grabbed his ankles under the mud," said

Max, shoving the hose down my pants.

"Ohhh, that's cold! Do you have to do that? I'm just going to get rolled and doughed in another minute anyway. I'll never make it. I can't!"

"You don't have to," said Daniela, shoving me into the booth. "Take off your clothes!"

"What?"

"Take off your clothes." It was Big David. He was standing in the booth with only his shorts on.

"Hurry up in there," Daniela shouted. "We only have a minute to go."

"Come on," said Big David. "It's my turn. I can't wait to get out there."

"What?" My skull must have been impacted with goo. I still didn't get it.

"Part of the plan," said Big David. "You took the first round, Lou took the second, and I'm taking the third."

So that was the plan! Nice of my pals to let me in on it!

There were just two more problems, the trophy and the Atomic Midget. "Has the Torpedo showed up yet?"

"Haven't seen her," said Big David. "No word about the trophy either."

"But I saw Joe Asher in the bleachers. Didn't he say anything?"

"Not to me."

I put on Big David's clothes and he put on the Masked Flea's uniform. It fit him a lot better than it fit me. We left the booth and hurried back to the arena.

"Walk taller," Max said to me. "You're Big David."

"Walk shorter," I called back to Big David, "You're the Masked Flea."

Daniela put my cape around Big David's shoulders. "Slow down. You're hurting. Wobble a bit and limp."

Big David played the role. He limped, cried out in pain, and slowly and reluctantly climbed into the ring. He hunched on the stool, looking small and frightened.

Butch pointed at him, laughing. "This one's mine, flea boy!" He bent over and wiggled his behind at the insignificant flea.

The Masked Flea smiled. You could see the change in his eyes, tiger eyes, intense, controlled, watching and waiting. Waiting for the bell that would open the tiger's cage. Butch the hunter had become Butch the prey.

Butch nodded at Slow Eddie and Slow Eddie rang the bell. The crowd applauded as Butch bounced across the ring and stood in front of the insignificant flea. "Come on, flea boy. You don't want to get beat up while you're still sitting down, do you?"

The tiger waited.

Butch turned his back on the Masked Flea. "How's this?" he taunted over his shoulder. "I want to be fair. You know, I won't even look. You got lucky once. See if you can do it again. Come on, shrimp. Give it your best shot before I tear you apart."

Big David stood up.

Butch looked over his shoulder. Something was different. Something was wrong. The flea looked taller, bigger, and he was smiling. Why would flea boy be smiling?

Big David stepped forward, wrapped his arm around

Butch, and pulled him to his chest so strongly it knocked the air out of him. "The flea is about to bite the rat," Big David whispered into Butch's ear.

Butch struggled but he couldn't break the Masked Flea's grip. He felt himself being lifted out of the mud. Suddenly, he was flying through the air and falling into the mud on the other side of the ring. He rolled through the mud and skidded into Slow Eddie. "Something's wrong," he gasped, spitting out mud. "Ring the bell! End the—"

He never finished the sentence. He was picked up again and found himself spinning around and around in the air. He landed with a thick splash on the other side of the ring. The Masked Flea fell on him and rolled him over and over, like a crocodile rolling its victim under water until it stopped moving.

Butch came up for air and crawled over to Slow Eddie. "Ring the bell, stupid. What are you waiting for?"

Slow Eddie kept pulling on the cord but nothing happened. Butch looked up and saw my friends sitting in the front row. Tony waved bye-bye to him with one hand and in the other hand he held up the bell clapper. He had removed it when Slow Eddie had gone to the bathroom. Slow Eddie could pull on that cord for the rest of his life and that bell was never going to make another sound.

Lindsey looked at Tony. "You bad boy," she said. "You know that's not fair."

Butch screamed as he was dragged back across the ring. He called out to the referee, but the referee was busy talking to a couple of men in striped shirts and several others in suits.

Butch had been folded up so many times, he was starting to look like a Swiss Army knife. I almost felt sorry for him. Big David was enjoying himself. I'd never seen him happier. The referee turned back to the match. He looked at his watch and then over at Slow Eddie who was frantically pulling on the bell cord.

Big David looked over at me. I nodded. Time to put an end to this terrible violence. The Masked Flea threw up his hands and headed for Butch.

Butch scooted through the mud as fast as he could, but not fast enough. Big David leaped into the air and landed on top of him, pinning him down.

"One, two, three," said the referee. He held up Big David's hand. "Winner of the third fall and new Champion of the Harvest Festival, the Masked Flea!"

The crowd cheered and yelled and hooted and whistled.

Butch rolled out of the ring and fell onto the dirt. Slow Eddie helped him up, but Butch pulled his arm away. "Stupid!" he snarled and limped off.

25

All Hail The Queen

A TV news helicopter circled Carpy Field. Below, several TV news trucks from as far away as San Francisco set up to record the big event. A couple of reporters were going over their lines while technicians lined up electrical cables and a series of microphones.

A volunteer crew from Central Valley Supply cleaned off the mud around the arena while another crew raised the sides by two feet and added fresh mud.

Max's dad was talking to the official referees from the professional World Mud Wrestling Federation. The men in suits were the president and secretary of the Federation and the superintendent of the school district. When the first rumor of the big bout had floated through their offices, no one had believed it. They were only convinced after talking with Superintendent Gordo of the school district, who verified it with his kindly and efficient school principal. Ms. Krunchensnap, or Big Mama the Eye Popper, had graciously agreed to come out of retirement for a final official bout. After some negotiations and several damage waivers, the superintendent accepted an agreement with the TV networks and the Wrestling Federation to sell the rights to film and broadcast for a fee of $500,000. He promised to donate $500 of that princely sum to the Harvest Festival.

"I don't know where the trophy is," Max's dad was saying. "I assume it will be here prior to the bout."

"You assume?" echoed Mr. Gordo.

"Where are the contestants?" asked Mr. Arnold, president of the Wrestling Federation.

"I assume they'll be here the same time the trophy shows up," Max's dad said nervously. "I assume."

"No problem," said Max who was standing next to his father.

"Who are you?" asked Mr. Gordo.

"This is my son." He smiled at Max. "Why don't you go sit down with your pals? This doesn't involve you."

Mr. Arnold surveyed the field. "This better not be some nutty rumor, because this is costing us a fortune. Does anyone actually know what's going on?"

The superintendent glanced across the field and into the stands. "They had better! Because I'm telling you now, I won't be made a laughingstock!"

I noticed my mom and dad sitting near Mr. and Mrs. Asher, chatting away amiably. Were they talking about me? No, they were smiling. I waved. My parents didn't see me, but Joe Asher did. He smiled.

There was a blast of trumpets from the main entrance of the playground, and the high school band marched onto the field playing *All Hail The Queen*. A dozen athletes waved flags on tall bamboo poles. The band was followed by the high school wrestling team unrolling a long red carpet. The gymnastic team bounced and tumbled down the carpet. Two girls from the girls' wrestling team threw white flower petals into the air and waved to the crowd.

Behind them, Big Mama the Eye Popper proudly strode in. She wore a skullcap that had a large bouncing eyeball attached to a thin spring. Her tights were green and her top was red. She had a long-sleeved, tight-fitting yellow shirt under the top and wore a cape with her symbol of a flying eye stitched on it.

She bowed and nodded, waving to the crowd. People who had been wandering around after the preliminary bout rushed to get back to their seats.

The officials hurried over and introduced themselves, followed by the newscasters. Everyone treated her like royalty. Kids and grown-ups surrounded Krunchensnap trying to get her autograph.

"Those guys in suits are coming over here," said Tony. "Who are they?"

"My father just told me," said Max. He sat down and explained about the officials. "They're waiting for the Torpedo and the trophy."

I put my face in my hands. My life was over.

"Isn't this fun?" Grandma David smiled. She gave Lindsey and Daniela each a gentle pat on the cheek. "Now I have girls, too," she said. "You two are so sweet."

Lindsey beamed. "I know."

The parade continued to the wrestling arena. A platform had been erected on two of the opposite corners of the ring. Over one flew the flag of the Flying Eyeball. The flagpole over the other was empty.

The parade stopped in front of the arena as the band continued to play. Big Mama paused in front of our little group of desperados. She smiled. My friends smiled. I felt like puking. She reached out, took my hand, and gently pulled me toward her.

"Congratulations, Mr. Russell, on winning the preliminary bout. You're always full of surprises."

She waved to the crowd, the smile never leaving her face. "Mr. Russell," she said through gritted teeth. "Look at all this. Isn't it truly beautiful? Who would have ever thought that someone like you and your little friends could have been responsible for all this, for providing me with this opportunity to get my trophy back." She looked at Tony, Max, Big David, and then back at me. She squeezed my hand. "Yes," she said, patting it. "Opportunity, that's the key word." She gave Daniela and Lindsey an icy smile. "I don't see the Torpedo. As a matter of fact, I don't see the trophy, either. Therefore I don't see any opportunity. Do you, Spoot?"

I didn't.

Big Mama waved to the crowd. "Oh, and one more thing." She smiled at the spectators. "If opportunity does show up, you'd better pray that I win. Come Monday morning, I want to see that trophy in my office sitting in its own little glass case where it belongs. And if it's not, Mr. Masked Flea, then nothing can save your sorry little you-know-what."

Big Mama continued to wave at her fans as she moved toward her corner of the ring. The high school wrestling team helped her up the short steps to a small platform where she continued to smile and wave to the crowd, soaking up the applause.

I looked at my pals and said, "I'm sorry. This was all my idea. A bad idea that just got worse."

"Forget it," said Lindsey. "We're in this together!"

We all turned and stared at her. "Wow," I said. "Thanks!" And I meant it.

"Oh, look," said Grandma David. "Here comes Mr. Lou. Yoohoo, Mr. Lou," she called out. "Come sit with us."

Lou was still dressed in the raincoat that was two sizes too big, sunglasses, and floppy hat. He looked happy. When he sat down, I leaned over and touched his sleeve.

"Thanks for fall number two," I said.

"Piece of cake." He smiled, took a plastic baggie from his coat pocket, and opened it.

"What is that? It looks like a ball of mashed bread."

"This? Angel food cake, I like to roll it into a ball, so it's easier to carry, very snackable. Listen, I got to ask you. Do you have a plan B?"

"You said the Torpedo would be here, right?"

"That was the feeling I got. I ran out in such a hurry, I left my pants behind."

I sighed and looked back toward the arena. "So I heard."

Lou ate the rest of his snack, crumbs falling like a light snow. He pointed at the end of our row. "A Plan B would be good." The rest of my crew leaned toward us, not only intently interested in what Lou was saying, but also looking toward where he was pointing.

I looked.

It was Father Mac. He was pushing a wheelchair with Mrs. Mac, alias the Torpedo the Atomic Midget, sitting in it with her leg sticking straight out and wrapped in a plaster cast.

"Move over kids," said Father Mac. He parked Mrs. Mac at the end of the bleacher and sat down next to her.

"This ought to be good," she said. "I love surprises!" She looked straight at me.

Father Mac patted Mrs. Mac on the arm. "Now, now, dear. Keep calm. Remember your marriage vows."

"See what I mean?" said Lou. "Plan B."

Gretchen squeezed in next to us along with a few other kids from our class. She handed me an envelope. "Mr. Asher said to give you this."

I opened the note and read it just loud enough for the few of us to hear.

Dear Mr. S. and friends,

I spoke with Chief MacCormick and told him everything I told you. My suspicions were correct about another key and the missing trophy. It was Mr. Seepage, the old principal who was fired last year. He kept his keys. The police searched his house and found the missing trophy and a lot of computers from our school and others as well.

I hope this will deliver me from my own stupidity.
The trophy is on its way.
J.

We froze. What? Mr. Seepage a thief? They found the trophy? In a sudden flurry of joy, we threw our arms around each other and gave each other high fives! One miracle deserves another, I thought. Why not?

Why not? Because the real Torpedo was sitting in a wheelchair with a broken leg. So much for another miracle.

The P.A. system crackled and the announcer said: "Will the Torpedo please step forward? We'd like to get the Battle of the Century started before the next century begins. Will the Torpedo please enter the ring?"

Mrs. Mac stared at the Eye Popper. Her hands grasped the arms of the wheelchair as though she were ready to launch herself into the ring despite having her leg in a cast. Father Mac whispered something in her ear and she seemed to relax a bit.

"I think we can cross the Torpedo off the list," Tony said.

I scrunched up my face and sealed my eyes shut, hoping that when I opened them, it would all be different. It wasn't.

"Maybe we should turn over the trophy and forget about everything else," said Lindsey. "Take our lumps."

"Our lumps?" I yelped. "Those lumps would be my lumps!"

Max looked over at Lou. "Plan B?"

Lou nodded.

"Come on," said Max. We followed Max and Lou into the Masked Flea's changing booth. What were they up to?

We heard the P.A. system again. "Will the Torpedo please make your presence known. Will you please step forward?" The announcer didn't sound quite as calm as the previous announcement. "Please!"

I pulled the tent flap back and checked out the crowd. People milled about and a few were leaving.

"We better do something and quick!"

Max pointed at Lou. "I'd like to introduce you to Plan B."

"What?"

Lou took off his coat. He was wearing the Torpedo's uniform underneath. He tossed the hat and sunglasses and slipped the Torpedo's mask over his head. He held out his arms. "Ta-da," he said. "Meet Plan B!"

"You're Plan B?" asked Lindsey.

I kept shaking my head. "No, no, no. She'll kill you. Give the uniform to me. I'll do it. I started all this. If anyone deserves to be crushed to death, it's me."

They all stared at me. Too dramatic? Or did they all know me better than I knew myself?

"We've been practicing," said Max. "We've been watching films of the Torpedo's old wrestling bouts. Lou's pretty good! He knows the Torpedo's moves. She was really light on her feet and very quick."

"I don't know," I said to Lou. "I don't want you to be hurt just because of one of my loony ideas."

"Will the rest of you guys be in my corner?" asked

Lou.

Everyone nodded. "Absolutely!"

"Then let's do it!"

"Okay, but then we have to make a grand entrance," I said. "Big David, go ask your brother for the drummers from the band, all the drummers! And bugles, blasting away, like an invading army!"

Big David took off.

"Meet us at the entrance on Tainter Street," I shouted. "Max, you stick with Lou and see that he gets anything he needs."

Max nodded.

Just as I was about to issue another order, Gretchen stuck her head in the tent.

"Can we help?" she asked. "We heard the rumors!"

"We?"

The rest of our class with the exception of Butch and Slow Eddie were right behind her. "Please? We want to help. It's our class too!"

"Great!" said Lindsey. "What we need is color! Pageantry!"

"My mother's dress shop!" someone said. "It's just across the street!"

"Let's go!"

"Tony, you take the rest of the class and see if you can borrow that gold spray-painted chair that was used in the school play. It's behind the Quonset hut." Tony grabbed a couple more students and they headed out.

Max covered Lou with a bright purple sheet that was crumpled up on a lawn chair. "Let's go out the back where no one will spot us." They disappeared under the tent.

I left the tent and walked back to the bleachers. Krunchensnap was hanging on the ropes staring at me, pretending to yawn. Her beady eyes followed me all the way back to where we'd been sitting. She grinned.

"Russell!" I heard someone say. It was Mrs. Mac. "I can't say I know much about this wrestling thing, but there's a rumor about Big Mama that not very many people know, a rumor about her one weakness." She put her hand on Father Mac's arm. He smiled and nodded. "Don't ask me how I heard this, but many years ago, in a different life, I did have a little interest in the wrestling circuit. The only time Big Mama was defeated was because she lost her temper. When she loses her temper, she makes mistakes."

"I'm not sure there is going to be another bout," I said.

Mrs. Mac stared at me for the longest time. "No? I think there will be. If anyone can make it work, it's you, Russell, with maybe a little help from unexpected sources."

"Unexpected sources?" I asked, confused.

She nodded knowingly and smiled. "Of course Russell, there is one other avenue you might consider."

"Yes?"

"Prayer, Russell, prayer!"

I started to say something, but stopped. We both heard it at the same time. Drums! Drums pounded out a fearful warning for all to hear. A storm was coming, a hurricane, a tornado, a jolting terrifying earthquake. Drums pounded out a frightful rhythm, a rousing challenge, marching closer and closer, louder and louder! Bugles blared and a cortège of supporters dressed in purple capes with yellow lightning bolts stitched on the back and wide-brimmed purple hats paraded past the bleachers.

Students from our class held a golden chair aloft and on it sat the Torpedo the Atomic Midget.

The crowd roared.

26
The Bout of the Century

Mr. Arnold, president of the World Wrestling Federation, and Superintendent Gordo breathed a sigh of relief as Police Chief MacCormick placed the stolen trophy on a table next to the officials. They waved to the cheering crowd.

Big Mama the Eye Popper didn't seem to notice the trophy, her murderous eyes fixed on the Torpedo. She sneered and growled as the Torpedo walked past her corner. She leaned over the ropes and shook her fist. "Cream puff!"

"Yum!" said the Torpedo. "I love cream puffs!"

"Yum?" said Big Mama. "That's all you can come up with, you little toad?"

The Torpedo folded his arms in confidence. "I know you are, but what am I?"

"You're a has-been, a never-was, a never-will-be, and an embarrassment to the wrestling profession!"

"I know you are," repeated the Torpedo, "but what am I?"

Big Mama rolled her eyes in exasperation. "Get with the program, peanut-head. Don't you understand I'm about to turn you into roadkill, you runtified pipsqueak?"

"I know you are, but what am I?"

Max pulled me closer and said, "I think we need an upgrade on the trash talk."

I nodded and whispered into the Torpedo's ear.

The Torpedo yawned and then glanced up at Big Mama. "Tell me," he said casually with a flip of his wrist, "You still have your Barbie Doll collection?"

Big Mama's eyes grew to the size of tennis balls. "What?"

"You've always been such a mama's girl," continued the Torpedo. "Do you still wear that frilly tutu at night and dance around your bedroom, pretending to be a ballerina singing *I Look So Lovely in Pink?*"

"AGGGGHHHH! You sawed-off midget!" screamed the Eye Popper. She leaped out of the ring, grabbed the trophy, and swung it at the Torpedo.

"Yikes!" cried Lou, dodging out of the way. He was quick. I'll give him that. He was so quick, he disappeared.

Big Mama swung again and again, slashing the air in search of the vanished Torpedo. One swing bounced the heavy trophy off of Mr. Arnold's forehead.

"Ahh," he cried out and spun backward, crumpling to the ground as his assistant rushed over to check his vital signs. One of the referees slapped an ice pack on the red, nasty lump that was already starting to bloom on his head.

Big Mama looked down at Mr. Arnold and then realized she was holding her stolen trophy. Her eyes grew wide and she hugged it tightly, kissing it. "Mine," she crooned happily. "Mine!"

Another referee tried to take the trophy and put it back on the table. "MINE!" shouted Big Mama, clutching it to her ample bosom.

"If you win!" said the referee. "Put it back or I'll disqualify you and declare the Torpedo the winner!"

Big Mama forced her fingers open and released the trophy. "Mine," she hissed.

The referee gestured toward the ring with his thumb. "You want the trophy, get in there and win the bout. One fall, no time limit, winner takes all!"

"No problem," she said, shoving the referee out of the way and climbing back into the ring. The crowd stood and applauded encouragement to their champion.

But where was her opponent?

Nowhere.

Tony knelt down and looked under the bleachers. "Where is he?"

"Is there a Plan C?" I squeaked.

"Don't worry," said Max. "It's all part of Plan B. We need to stall. Where's Big David?"

"I'm standing next to you,"

"Oh," said Max, "sorry, it's all these purple capes and hats. We're all starting to look alike. Whose idea was this?"

"Not mine," I said. "I didn't even know about Plan B! Maybe if I had... " I stopped in mid-sentence. Obviously, no one was listening. "Where's Tony?"

"Over here," said Tony, "next to Max." They were both signaling to Big David who was standing in front of the band with his brother and the band major.

The band major turned and struck up the full high school band. They played the *Star Spangled Banner*. Everyone stood up and faced the flag, including Big Mama.

When the anthem was over, someone raised a banner over the Torpedo's corner. It unfurled to show a circle with a sledgehammer over an eyeball.

The crowd loved it.

Max's father made a few announcements followed by the superintendent who introduced Mr. Arnold. Mr. Arnold held an ice pack on his head as he thanked the organizers of the Harvest Festival. My mother's name was mentioned several times. She stood proudly with the other PTA members and they all waved politely to the cameras and the crowd.

The Federation announcer stood in the middle of the wrestling ring, wearing waders. He pulled down the suspended microphone and the spectators grew quiet.

"And now for the Mud Wrestling Championship of the World! One fall, no time limit, first to pin her opponent takes the trophy for all time. In this corner, we have Big Mama the Eye Popper," he said, pointing in her direction. She leaped off the ropes and danced about, turning toward the crowd with her arms raised over her head, fists clasped together pumping the air triumphantly. The fans yelled and stomped their feet.

"And in this corner, we have, ah, in this corner we have…"

"Where's Plan B?" I said, nervously.

"And in this corner we have…"

Suddenly, out of the middle of the arena, an iron grate flew into the air as though it had been shot out of a cannon. It was followed by a figure spinning like a propeller, rising higher and higher, spraying mud across Big Mama's face and splattering the first three rows of fans. The figure seemed to hover in the air for a moment, spreading its arms like airplane wings, its cape flapping in the breeze.

The circular grate fell back into the mud, splashing more muck on Superintendent Gordo.

"…Torpedo the Atomic Midget!" the announcer shouted.

The fans screamed, blew horns and whistles, and stomped their feet so loudly, it felt like the bleachers were going to collapse.

"Are you ready?" asked the announcer.

Big Mama pulled on the ropes and gnashed her teeth while Torpedo the Atomic Midget sat in our corner on a stool, eating biscotti from a bag.

"Where'd you get that?" I asked.

"Father Mac," said Lou the Torpedo. "He's a great baker. He can cook, too! Want one?"

"Heads up," said Max. "We're getting serious!"

The Atomic Midget took another bite.

The announcer checked the referee, nodded, then climbed out of the ring, and sat down in front of the bell. He pulled on the cord to start the bout, but nothing happened.

The bell clapper was still in Tony's pocket.

Tony handed it to Max, who handed it to his father, who handed it over to the announcer, who scratched his head. He screwed the bell clapper back in and pulled the cord.

The bell rang and a roar went up from the crowd.

Big Mama shot out of her corner like a starving Tyrannosaurus Rex splashing its way through the muck toward its next meal. She roared as she reached out, her thick fingers opening and closing, ready to grasp her prey.

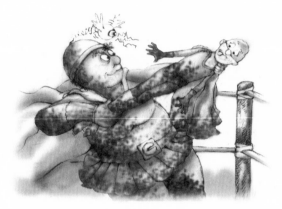

27

The Eye Popper Stretch

There was a thunderous crash as Big Mama smashed into the stool and bent the corner pipe halfway to the arena floor. The Torpedo cried out and dove into the mud. Big Mama spun around and went after the Torpedo. She caught him by the ankle and whipped him out of the mud.

She grabbed the other end of the Torpedo and lifted him over her head. Then she gave her opponent Big Mama's famous Eye Popper Stretch.

"Oh! Ow!" cried the Torpedo. "Let go!"

"Let go?" asked Big Mama. She stretched him as far as she could, one thick arm pulling back on his head and the other muscular arm pulling on his feet. "No problemo!" she said. She pointed his head toward a tall light fixture, pulling tighter and tighter, and then let go. He shot into the sky like a rubber band, his cape fluttering in the wind, arced over and over, and landed in the middle of a salami sandwich Grandma David was preparing for Little David.

Mayonnaise, lettuce, and slices of French bread flew everywhere. The salami bounced down the bleachers and rolled into a clump of mud. Grandma David stood up, glaring at Big Mama. "That wasn't very nice," she said. "Little David, you help the contestant back to where she belongs."

Little David helped Lou untangle himself. "You okay?" he asked.

The Torpedo picked off a slice of pickle that was stuck to his chest and ate it. "Strange," he said. "I feel taller." Little David ushered the Torpedo back to his corner of the arena.

Grandma David was furious. She marched up to the wrestling ring. Big Mama was swaggering through the mud, taking in the applause when she noticed the old lady with the salami. She leaned over the ropes. "Go back to your seat!"

"Don't tell me what to do, you fat blimp. You got mud on my salami. What's the matter with you? Somebody should teach you some manners!"

"Oh, yeah," mocked the Eye Popper. "And who's that going to be? You, you old bag?"

"Yeah!" said Grandma David and she shoved the salami into Big Mama's face.

"YEOH!" cried Big Mama. "My eye, my eye! I'm blind!"

Little David took his grandmother's arm and led her back to her seat. She stopped suddenly, turned, and shouted back toward the arena. "You're lucky I didn't bring my chair!"

Big Mama rubbed her face and shook her head, blinking and straining to see. The Torpedo climbed back into the ring.

"Now!" Max shouted.

The Torpedo growled, hunched up his narrow shoulders, and then tackled Big Mama behind her knees, felling her like a redwood tree. She collapsed in the mud, her thick legs kicking in the air, and screamed a string of curses no child should hear. The mud spilled over the sides, carrying a referee up and over the side of the ring and into the base of the bleachers where another official hosed him off.

Just as it looked like the Torpedo had the advantage, Big Mama broke the hold, twisted, and flipped her thick legs around his neck. She squeezed and flipped him into the mud.

Mud splattered into our corner. I felt like I was at Marine World, watching Shamu the killer whale do a rolling dive.

Together, the wrestlers disappeared under the mud and then Shamu breached out of the mud, arching high into the air with the Torpedo's shorts clutched between her teeth. The Torpedo was still in them.

"Foul!" cried the Torpedo before disappearing into the mud again.

"Big Mama," yelled the crowd. "The eye, the eye, the eye," they chanted over and over, hooting and whistling.

"The Torpedo," shouted another part of the crowd. "Crush the eye, crush the eye." They blew air horns and jeered at the eye supporters.

Big Mama jumped up and down in the middle of the ring, trying to stomp the Torpedo into submission. She dropped to her knees and plunged her fist into the mud, searching for her buried enemy.

"Is my butt still there?" asked a voice behind us.

We all turned at the same time to see a gob of mud standing there. "Lou?"

"I mean it wasn't very big to begin with, but now? I think she bit off a chunk. Take a look." The Torpedo bent over. "Is it still there?"

"Lou?"

"What?"

"What are you doing out here?" asked Max.

"Taking a break," explained the glob of mud.

"There are no breaks," said Tony.

"No? Well, anytime you want to jump in the ring with Big Mama and get your butt chewed off, let me know."

"I'll pass," said Tony.

"Uh oh," said Max.

We all looked up. Big Mama the Eye Popper was hanging on the ropes, staring down at us. "There you are, you little featherweight! You spineless, puny-muscled, good-for-nothing, disgusting loser!"

The Eye Popper leaped over the ropes. We scattered in every direction, abandoning our vows of friendship.

She snatched the glob of mud and flipped him back into the ring. A nasty grin spread across her face as she climbed back over the ropes. She reached down and tugged on her opponent's ankles. She pulled and pulled. The harder she pulled, the longer the legs stretched and then, with a weird smacking noise, she jerked the Torpedo out of the mud, turned him right side up, and put him in a bear hug. She squeezed and squeezed. She squeezed so hard, his head and his feet, the two ends of his body, got bigger, like squeezing a balloon in the middle, and then, she tossed him over her shoulder like so much discarded trash.

The Torpedo pulled himself up and dizzily wobbled over to our corner. "Look at me!" he said. "I am taller. Isn't that great? My back feels better, too!"

"It's good to always look on the positive side," I said.

"Right," said Tony.

Daniela shook her head. "I think he's a little dizzy."

"No kidding," said Lou. "Guess what?"

We all looked at each other, waiting for one of us to come up with the answer.

"What?"

"Time for Plan C."

28
Plan C

The Torpedo headed to the middle of the ring and fell to his knees, reaching into the mud.

"What's he doing?" Tony asked.

"I don't get it," said Max. "What's Plan C?"

Big Mama watched the Torpedo cautiously, slowly circling him with outstretched arms, waiting for some kind of trick.

There was a sucking noise and Lou disappeared. Mud oozed down the hole and slowly drained away.

He was gone.

Big Mama stopped circling. She looked down into the dark passage and grinned.

She waved at the referees and pointed at the hole. "She ran away!" she shouted. "I win! The trophy's mine!"

She raised her arms in victory and then with clenched fists, she let out a King Kong roar. She beat on her chest and howled. From far away coyotes howled back. Cats arched their backs and hissed. Rats were seen running down the street, having abandoned dark cellars and old woodpiles.

The crowd was silent, stunned, frozen, while Big Mama strode around the ring, waving and pointing at the trophy, shouting "Mine! Mine! Mine!"

We didn't know what to say.

What could we do?

"That's Plan C?" asked Lindsey. "Running away?"

"She won. So are we off the hook?" asked Max. "Or does she have something else she can pin on us? Maybe she knows we were at her house the other night."

"No," I said. "And I don't think Lou ran away."

Big Mama knelt down and put her head down the hole. She let out a blood-curdling screech that sent a flock of starlings soaring into the air. "COWARD!" she screamed.

Something screamed back, something from deep under the ground. Something from the sewers. Something bigger than the Torpedo. Something bigger than Big Mama.

We took a step backward.

"What was that?" I whispered.

We looked at each other wide-eyed.

The crowd stood up, anxious, talking to each other without taking their eyes off the arena. Was that the end of the bout? Was this part of the Harvest Festival? Had the Torpedo run away? Was Big Mama the Eye Popper the winner?

A second high-pitched squeal echoed from the hole

followed by a snuffling sound. Two large beady black eyes peered out.

Big Mama stood up quickly and jumped back.

A hairy head covered in muddy algae appeared, its eyes blinking in the strong afternoon sun. The creature let out another squeal as it struggled to pull itself up and out of the shaft. When it managed to free itself, it stood up on its hind legs and cried out.

The referee scrambled out of the ring. Everyone in the lower tiers climbed to the top rows, too scared to be any closer, but too curious to run away. News photographers snapped pictures. A helicopter hovered above the arena. Another photographer videotaped the event for the local TV station.

The creature looked about. When it saw us at the side of the ring, it let out another squeal and wobbled toward us. It was carrying a muddy glob of something in its mouth. When it stopped at the ropes, it sniffed the air. It looked at Tony and me, twitched its nose, and spit the glob at our feet.

"Yuck," said Lindsey. "Poor Lou."

The creature cried out a fearful scream that startled everyone. Big Mama had picked it up and held it over her head, its thick legs kicking furiously in the air. "I know who you are!" she shouted. "The Yonkers Yeti! That coward, the Atomic Midget, sent you! It doesn't matter! No one defeats Big Mama the Eye Popper! That trophy is mine, do you hear? MINE!"

She tossed the whimpering creature into a corner of the ring. It cried out again and started chewing through the ropes to get away. A few mothers gathered up their children and ran off toward the parking lot. But most, either out of fear or curiosity, couldn't help themselves. They had to watch. The press kept talking into their microphones and the photographers kept snapping pictures.

A screech echoed from the hole and another, larger creature emerged, calling to the first.

"A tag-team!" shouted the Eye Popper. "The Yeti Twins! Two against one! No matter! No one defeats Big Mama!"

She reached over the side of the arena and grabbed the nozzle of the fire hose and hit the second creature over the head. It moaned, then rose up on its hind legs and squealed. It was half again taller than Big Mama. It wobbled toward the smaller creature, squealing softly. When the Eye Popper hit it over the head again, the creature cried out in pain.

"Come on, hairball! Fight like a man!" she cried and whacked the creature again.

The creature stopped, turned, and picked up Big Mama. It carried her to the edge of the ring and tossed her out.

"I'm not done yet!" Big Mama yelled. "What you need is a bath!"

She reached over and turned on the fire hose valve.

"NO!" shouted the fire chief. "The nozzle! No one's holding the nozzle!" He and another fireman climbed out of the stands and ran toward the hose. But it was too late. A rush of water filled the fire hose and it snapped back and forth, flailing up and down, showering everyone in the stands like a thunderstorm. It lashed across the arena and the playground, knocking down the tents, the ticket stand, and anything in its path. It knocked Big Mama down as she tried to climb back into the ring. She rolled over and over. As she rolled past the trophy table, she snatched the trophy and hurtled across the playground.

Two more firefighters and the police chief jumped on the hose and forced it down while the fire chief shut off the valve. Everywhere you looked, there was water. Everyone was soaked, including us.

"Was that Plan C?" I asked.

"Look at my clothes!" Lindsey moaned. She glared at me. "This is your fault, Sprowt. You and the rest of your gang."

"Oh, my," said Tony, looking at his feet.

"What?"

Tony pointed at the ground.

David looked at Tony. "What? Your shoes?"

"They're on your feet," said Max. "Isn't that where they're supposed to be?"

Tony bent over and picked up a pair of shoes. "Not those shoes, these shoes. They brought my shoes back."

"Who?"

Tony pointed toward the arena.

The two creatures stood in the center of the ring, dripping water from their clean, soft brown fur. They made sniffing noises and gurgled, their black eyes staring at Tony.

Tony nodded.

"Mr. and Mrs. Wiggles."

29
Winners And Losers

Monday morning I walked to school, wondering what was in store for us. I was happy to be alive to tell the tale, except the tale wasn't quite over. No, Ms. Krunchensnap was waiting, waiting to render a verdict on yours truly and his friends. Would she keep her word and free us from the Manure List, or would she laugh hysterically and sentence us all to hard labor on Devil's Island?

I crossed the street and walked into the schoolyard. My friends were standing at the edge of Carpy Field, watching volunteers take down the booths and load them onto pickup trucks. The County Office of Education had a big flatbed truck parked in the center of the field. Men were folding up the bleachers and stacking them on the truck with a forklift. A city work crew in bright orange vests was sealing up the drain hole in the middle of the field with a heavy iron grate.

Max waved me over. "Hard to believe it's over," he said.

"Is it?"

"Is it what?"

"Over?"

I pulled out a folded newspaper from my back pocket and held it up in front of them. "Read the headline!"

Daniela snatched the paper from me and read it out loud. "Famous Wrestler Disappears in Wild Bout of the Century, Winner Uncertain, Decision to Follow." She waved the paper in the air. "What's that supposed to mean?"

"Maybe it means Ms. Krunchensnap didn't win and they'll have to have another bout," Big David suggested.

"No way!" Lindsey shouted. "I'm not going through that again! All I want is to get off Russell's Manure List!"

"It's not just my list," I said defensively.

Max looked at his watch. "And in a few minutes, we're going to find out what happens to it and us."

Tony pointed at the newspaper. "What's that other headline say?"

Daniela read the headline, "Giant Short-Tailed Rats Invade Town Harvest Festival!"

Lindsey shook her head. "Can't they tell the difference between a rat and a gopher?"

"Hamsters," said Tony. "Mr. and Mrs. Wiggles are hamsters."

"Hamsters, gophers, what's the difference?"

Tony looked at me.

"How are they?"

"Fine," said Tony. "They're in our backyard, giving the neighborhood kids piggyback rides. I hope we can keep them."

"What about the zoo?" asked Max, looking at his watch again.

"No zoos!" said a familiar voice.

We all turned. It was Lou. He was wearing the old shirt with his name on it, his big floppy hat, sunglasses, high-top tennis shoes, and bib overalls with the cuffs rolled up. "No zoos!" He waved a warning finger.

"Lou!" we cheered. We were glad to see him. But there was something different about him. I couldn't stop staring.

"What?"

Suddenly I realized what it was. I wasn't looking down at him! I was looking up! He was six inches taller than me. "You grew!"

"Stretched." He grinned.

"Thanks for helping us."

Everyone joined in and thanked Lou for all he'd done for us. Even Lindsey gave him a hug.

"What are friends for?" He blushed a pale orange.

The bell rang.

As we walked toward the classrooms, Lou called out behind us. "After school," he shouted. "The war room. I have something to show you. You won't believe it!"

We waved and went into the building.

Mrs. P was standing in front of the room, patiently waiting as we filed in and took our seats.

"Good morning," she said. "You'll be happy to know that Miss Sally is recovering nicely, but I'm afraid she's not quite ready to return to the classroom. She'll be attending a special clinic for recovering substitute teachers." She looked at the clock on the wall. "Your new teacher is running a little late. It was a very big weekend for everyone, so Ms. Krunchensnap has asked me to tell you and the rest of the students not to talk today. No noise, especially around her office. She's canceled recess, so you're to stay in the classroom all day. She has declared this a rainy day."

"But the sun is out," said Slow Eddie.

I looked across the aisle at him. "You are so sharp!"

"It's their fault," Butch protested. "Poor Ms. Krunchensnap tries so hard. All she wants is a little peace. It's their fault for what happened at the Harvest Festival."

"Yeah," said Slow Eddie. "They was at the roots. Will they be sent to prison, Mrs. P, for perspiring to commits deeds?"

"We was Ms. Krunchensnap's best students. We had to report those guys' misbehaviors. Is Ms. Krunchensnap dead? 'Cause murder is like, serious, Mrs. P."

"Thank you for that insight, Percy."

Big David smiled at Butch. Butch touched a bruise on his cheek and looked away nervously.

"May I finish?" asked Mrs. P.

We waited.

"I was only kidding about recess," she said. "The Harvest Festival was very successful or so I'm told. I'm only here for two reasons. One, to wait for the teacher to arrive. She should be here any minute."

"Is it Miss Butters?" Gretchen asked.

Mrs. P shook her head. "No, it is not Miss Butters. And two," she continued, "Ms. Krunchensnap wishes to see Russell, Tony, Max, David, Daniela, and Lindsey in her office."

We all moaned

"When?" I asked.

"Right about now."

"Yes!" Butch smirked.

We left the classroom and walked down the long hall we knew all too well.

Other than Lindsey complaining, no one said much.

The door was open to Krunchensnap's office. We knocked anyway. "Enter," announced a raspy voice.

The first thing we saw was the trophy sitting on her desk.

"You won!"

Ms. Krunchensnap sat behind her desk. Her head was bandaged, her right cheek was swollen, and her left arm was in a sling. "Sort of," she said.

Everyone was waiting for me to say something. Why me? Why not? I had the habit. "What do you mean, sort of?"

"What do I mean? I mean the World Mud Wrestling Federation officials called me this morning to tell me they decided to call it a draw. Since neither opponent was pinned for a count of three, the trophy reverts to me. I keep it until the Torpedo reappears."

"But the Torpedo may never come back," I said, pointing out the obvious.

"Fine by me," she said. "I'll still have the trophy. I

have the feeling that the Torpedo isn't very far away, that she's watching us this very minute, waiting for a chance to get her hands on my trophy."

She looked out the window for a moment and then pulled down the blinds.

The phone rang and Krunchensnap picked it up. "What? No. I already have somebody! Yes, to replace Miss Sally. Fine, I guess. I already talked to you about this! What?" Krunchensnap covered the phone. "Is Mrs. P in the classroom?"

We nodded.

"Is the teacher there yet?"

We shook our heads.

Krunchensnap uncovered the phone. "Why? Because I haven't had time to look for a new custodian, that's why. I was busy raising half a million dollars for you this weekend, remember?" She hung up the phone. "Superintendents!" she groused.

"I know a great custodian," I said.

Everyone stared at me with that 'now what?' expression I often got from my friends.

Big David nodded. "Mr. Lou."

I returned the nod. "Mr. Lou."

"I'm not interested in another one of your scams, Mr. Russell." She picked up a piece of paper from her desk.

"He'll work for half of what you paid Mr. Asher!"

That got her attention. "Really?"

"Really!"

"Tell him to meet me in my office. I'll try him out for a week. If he works out, I'll hire him full time."

She looked at me like a bug under a microscope. "Now this last item on my morning's agenda. The famous smoking manure list!"

I didn't dare take a breath.

"We had a deal, Mr. Russell. And I suppose Saturday's World Wrestling Championship fits our agreement concerning the term opportunity." She took out the black box and dumped the contents, picked up the manure list, tore it in half, and let it float slowly down, down, down into the wastebasket. Then she slid all the other cards off the desk into the trash as well. She stared sadly at the basket. "Such a shame," she sighed. She glanced back at the trophy and a weak little smile forced itself across her face.

"As of this morning, we are even, Mr. Sprowt." She looked right into my eyes. "As for tomorrow, we'll just have to wait and see. The world is full of surprises. Now get out."

We walked back to the classroom filled with a sense of relief. Top of the world! We gave each other high five's, hugs, and pats on the back.

Mrs. P was waiting in the doorway.

We took our places. I looked at the teacher and then back at Mrs. P standing by the open doorway. She was right, our teacher's name wasn't Miss Butters. It was Mrs. Asher.

And there she was, with that sweet smile on her face, and here we were, with smiles on ours.

A Last Word or Two

Ms. Krunchensnap never changed one bit. Not one iota. Not a single speckaronni.

When Mr. Gordo, the superintendent, was fired for spending the Harvest Festival proceeds on a new vacation house in Lake Tahoe, the Eye Popper was asked if she wanted the position. "Ha!" she snapped, "If I wanted to take a leave of absence, I'd take the job!"

It was also rumored that Mrs. Mac was the Torpedo. Some of us knew the truth about that one. And now you do, too. Keep it to yourself.

Mr. Lou did get the custodial job. He transformed the school overnight into the cleanest, neatest, most polished school in the district. That's not a rumor.

There was a rumor that Mr. Lou was more than one person. People said that at night when the lights were on, people could see Mr. Lou at both ends of the building at the same time. A rumor spread that Mr. Lou had cousins who moved into other schools, older schools, schools that had pipes that rattled and sinks that made burpy noises, like your school, for instance. Hey! It's only a rumor.

Oh, and one more thing, remember that meeting in the war room that Lou wanted to have after school? Would you like to know what happened and what he found out?

Of course you would.

I'd tell you, only you wouldn't want me to spread another rumor, would you? But you know what they say, where there's smoke...

Denys Cazet has published more than fifty books for young readers, including the popular *Never Spit on Your Shoes,* winner of the California Young Reader Medal. His most recent book, *Minnie & Moo: Hooves of Fire* garnered a Kirkus Star and made their Best Children's Book list for 2014. Mr. Cazet, for years a school librarian, lives in Pope Valley, California. He has never been a mud wrestler but is an avid fan of spreading rumors with friends, neighbors, and the family cat, Felix.

Other Books
by
Denys Cazet

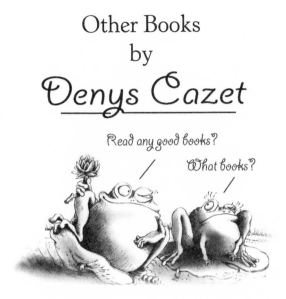

Read any good books?

What books?

Minnie & Moo: Hooves of Fire

Minnie & Moo Go to Paris

Minnie & Moo: The Seven Wonders of the World

The Perfect Pumpkin Pie

Will You Read to Me?

Snail and Slug

Bob and Tom